MARVEL

BLACK
PANTHER
RULES!

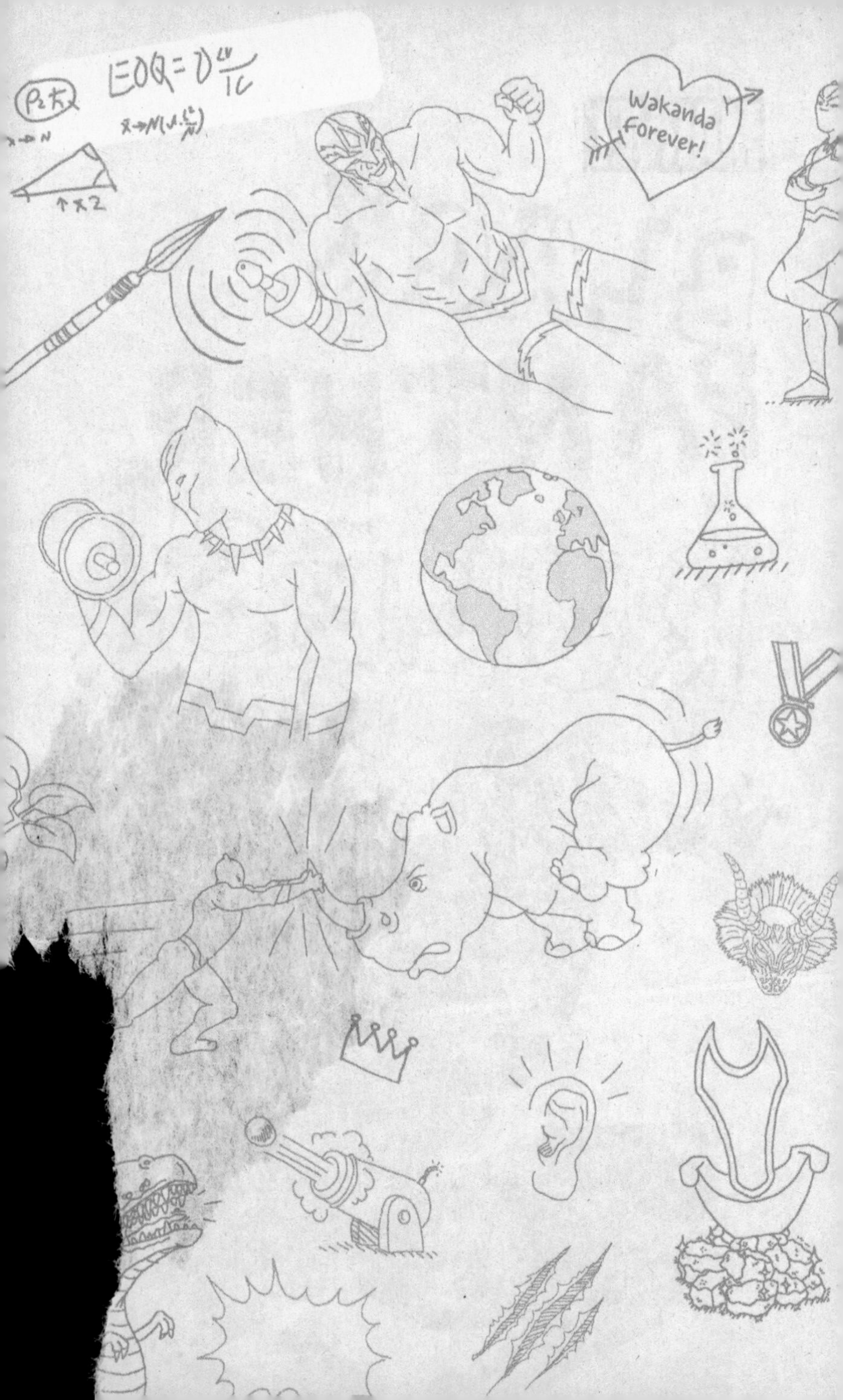
Wakanda Forever!

MARVEL

BLACK PANTHER

RULES!

written by
Billy
Wrecks

CONTENTS

Who is the Black Panther?   6

Keeping it in the family   36

So tell me more about this Wakanda!   54

Wait! who would dare take on the BLACK PANTHER?! 68

Allies and Avengers to the rescue 82

Glossary 122

Index 124

Acknowledgments 128

You rule!

Wakanda Forever!

who is the Black Panther?

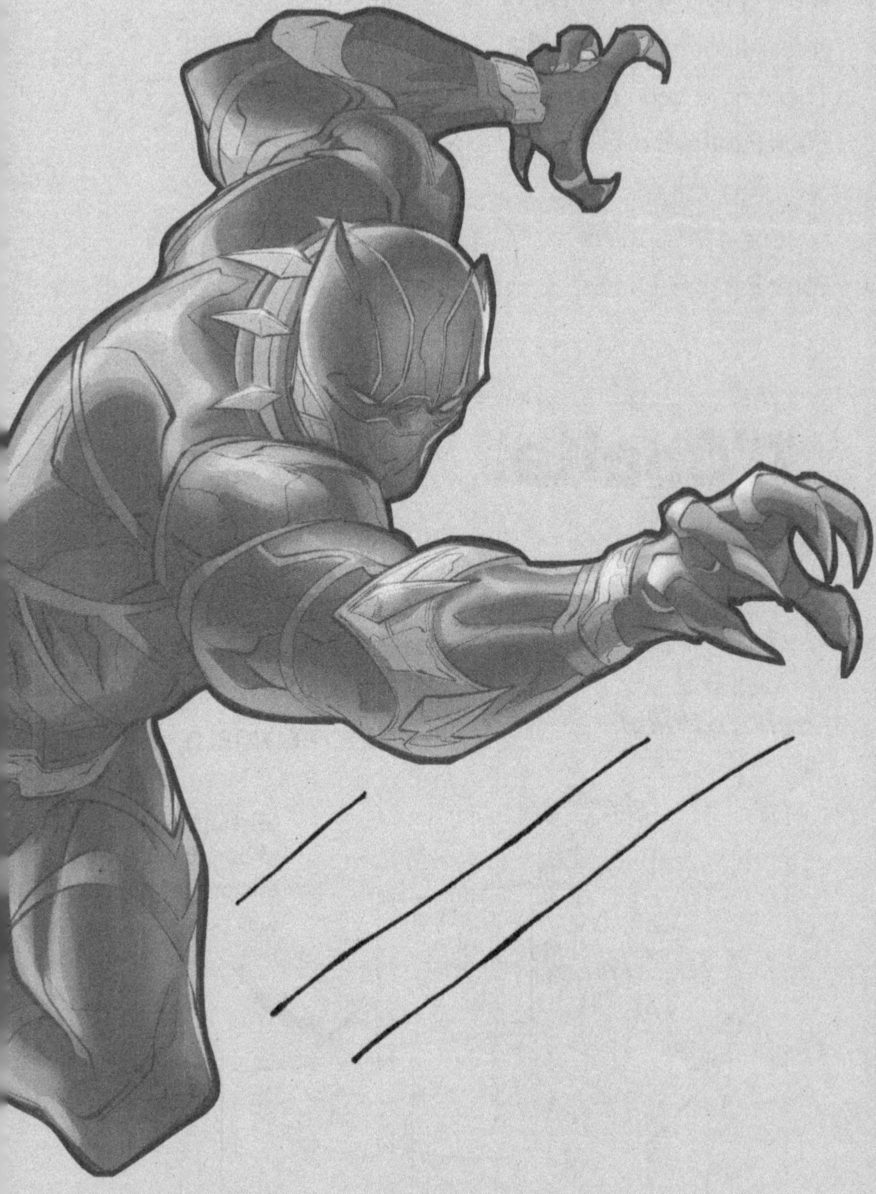

Black Panthers are the **kings** and **protectors** of the great nation of **Wakanda.** There have been **many** Black Panthers over the centuries, but the most famous is the current Black Panther, known as

T'Challa.

As **king,** T'Challa has helped turn Wakanda into one of the most technologically **advanced** countries **IN THE WORLD.**

Look at me multitasking!

Whew! And you thought having just one or two hobbies was tough!

As **Black Panther,** he has **protected** his **homeland** from internal and external foes.

In addition, as a member of Earth's **MIGHTIEST** team of **SUPER HEROES,** the

Avengers,

he has saved the **world** again and again!

"Just saved the world again" pose

Avengers symbol

Being a king **isn't** just sitting on a throne all day, dripping with jewels. T'Challa has to put up with constant **internal** strife. There's always some distant **relative** who says **THEY** have a claim to the throne, or a tribal elder or council member **questioning** your decisions. (Which is **SUPER** annoying!)

Sometimes there's a pesky little **sister** getting in your way. Okay, she makes up for it by inventing **SUPER-COOL GADGETS** and **TECH.** And then there are always, **ALWAYS,** people like **Killmonger** who are just out to destroy you.

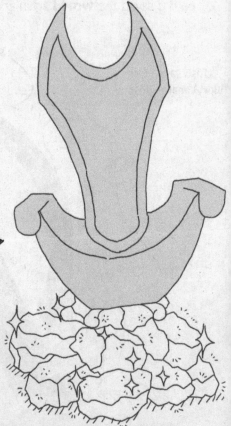

The Wakandan throne does not LITERALLY sit on a mountain of Vibranium ... but there is a LOT of it!

And if that wasn't enough trouble, Wakanda sits on top of the biggest pile of the **MOST VALUABLE** metal on Earth. It's called **Vibranium** (more on this later), and villains such as Klaw, Kraven the Hunter, and even **aliens** are always trying to get their evil hands* on it.

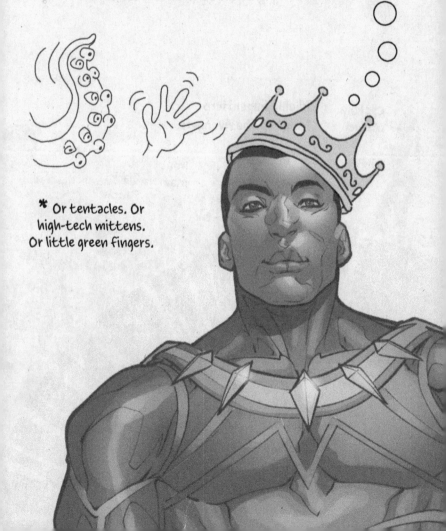

I wish this crown would fit under my mask!

* Or tentacles. Or high-tech mittens. Or little green fingers.

On top of being **KING** of a whole nation, Black Panther is also a **Super Hero.** And Super Hero teams like **THE AVENGERS** are **FULL** of **DRAMA.** Someone is always losing their super-powers, then getting them back, or leaving the team, then rejoining it, or even **dying** and then coming **back to life!** See? **Drama!**

Captain Marvel

Mighty Super Hero team—up The Avengers:

Hulk

Iron Man

Black Panther

Hawkeye

Thor

Ant-Man

And let's face it, **the Avengers** are comprised of gods, giant green rage machines, and handsome billionaire industrialists, so the personalities are

BIG.

And don't forget, where there are Super Heroes, there are **Super Villains** doing all sorts of evil things like trying to **take over the world** or collecting multicolored (and very powerful) magic gems … So Black Panther has a **LOT** to deal with!

Wasp

Falcon

War Machine

Captain America

Black Widow

SPOILER ALERT: These heroes really know how to party.

Being a Super Hero does have its perks!

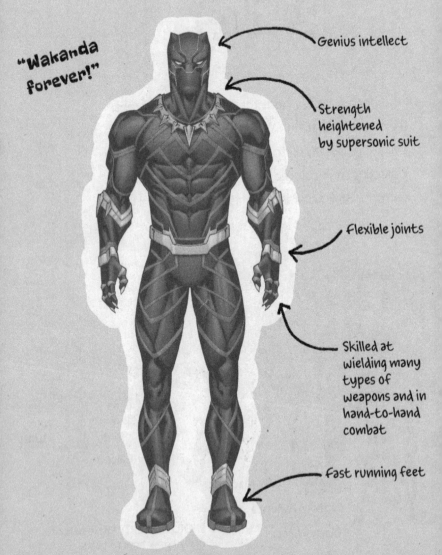

Genius intellect

Strength heightened by supersonic suit

Flexible joints

Skilled at wielding many types of weapons and in hand-to-hand combat

Fast running feet

"Wakanda forever!"

Despite some of the **issues** with being a Super Hero, it's still a pretty cool job. As the Black Panther, T'Challa has some amazing **Super-powers,** such as enhanced **STRENGTH** and **SPEED.** He gets to wear a

high-tech battlesuit

that protects him from all kinds of physical damage.

He's also highly **intelligent** (although his sister Shuri would say not as intelligent as her!). And let's face it, he gets to hang out with heroes such as Captain America and go on adventures all over the world, outer space, and even other **DIMENSIONS!**

No need to show off, we get it, you're strong!

But being a **King** isn't *so bad* either …

T'Challa may have the usual **problems** that come with being a ruler, but an entire **NATION** of people look up to him and

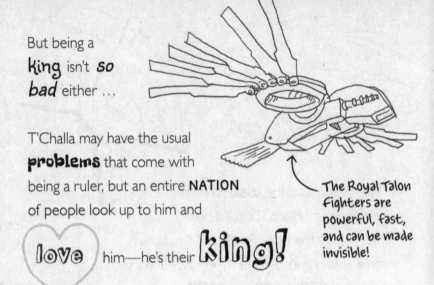

love him—he's their **king!**

The Royal Talon Fighters are powerful, fast, and can be made invisible!

Wakanda has the most **ADVANCED TECHNOLOGY** in the world, and as king, T'Challa has unlimited access to an awesome array of futuristic **gadgets, high-tech gear,** and technology including **jets, computers, battlesuits,** and **weapons.** Even the capital city, Birnin Zana, looks pretty high-tech and snazzy.

Wakanda's capital city skyline

On top of state-of-the-art **TALON FIGHTERS,**
DRAGON FLYERS, and **ARMORED WAR RHINOS,***
T'Challa also has fierce, all-female royal bodyguards,
known as the **Dora Milaje,** on his side!

***** Take that,
KILLMONGER!

Now this is what
I call traveling
in style!

Zoom!

Hover bike: Great for
battle, but hard to park. →

T'Challa is only the **LATEST** king to wear the mantle of the Black Panther. He is one of many in a **long line** of Black Panthers that stretch back over **10,000 years.**

That's a LONG time! Ready for some brief (and weird) history? Let's go. About 10,000 years ago, a **meteorite**

CRASHED

into the region of Africa that would become known as **WAKANDA.** The meteorite left behind an **amazing space metal** called **vibranium.**

Early Wakandans used this metal to enhance their weapons ... but **radiation** from the metal had strange effects on animals and plants. It even turned some people into MONSTERS!

At the same time, a **MIGHTY WARRIOR** named **BASHENGA** rose up to bring order to the chaos. He would become the first ever Black Panther ...

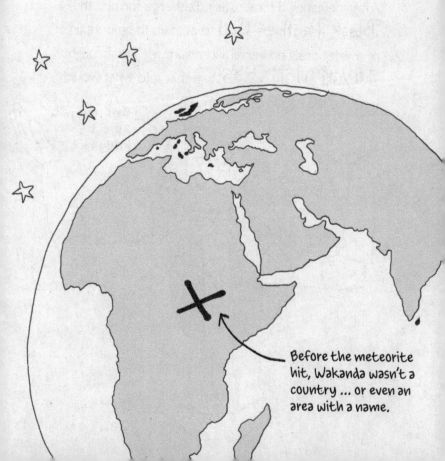

Before the meteorite hit, Wakanda wasn't a country ... or even an area with a name.

While the new Vibranium-formed **monsters ROAMED THE LAND,** warrior Bashenga **prayed** to the **Panther Goddess BAST,** who bestowed on him the power to defeat them. These powers made him **pantherlike: strong, stealthy, and fast ...**

After defeating the monsters, Bashenga formed the **Black Panther Cult** to protect the mountain of mysteriously powerful Vibranium. He also brought **several tribes** together into what would become the nation of Wakanda.

Bast: not just
a pretty,
kitty face

Other cults formed around the **mutated creatures** and survived through the centuries, such as the **WHITE APE Cult.** There is also a **CROCODILE Cult** and a **LION Cult.**

Phew, we're nearly up to date! **Nowadays,** Black Panther is the **TITLE** bestowed on the **CHIEF OF WAKANDA** and **LEADER** of the Panther Cult. Through a series of *grueling* physical and mental **TESTS** also known as **TRIALS,** a candidate proves that they are *worthy of the title.*

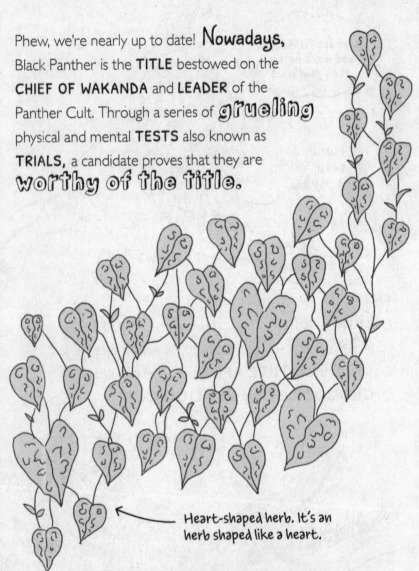

← Heart-shaped herb. It's an herb shaped like a heart.

Then with the **BLESSING OF BAST,** the worthy warrior is allowed to drink a *potion* made from a magical **heart-shaped herb.**

This **HERB** grows in Wakanda and was also affected by the Vibranium. Consuming it grants a person **enhanced** physical **STRENGTH** and **SPEED**.

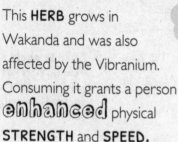

Mmm, delicious!

Every Black Panther for the last **10,000 years** has had to pass these tests and drink the potion— **INCLUDING** T'Challa.

In **more recent years** T'Challa's grandfather, **AZZURI,** fought alongside the hero **CAPTAIN AMERICA** to keep the villain **Red Skull** and the Nazis out of Wakanda.

I may be as old as T'Challa's grandpa but I can still run faster than you!

Captain America: loyal Avenger and friend of Wakanda. Original shield, before he discovered circles, was a triangle.

But by helping other nations, Wakanda's **greatest secret** was not a secret anymore! Rumors leaked out, and soon **the US** and **Germany** found out about the Vibranium. How **FIERCELY** would Wakanda FIGHT to protect its secret? People were about to find out ...

T'Challa's **father, T'chaka,** was both a **GREAT KING** and Black Panther. He **successfully kept** the outside world from encroaching on their nation and getting their hands on the precious metal. **UNTIL ...**

This isn't just a smartphone!

Klaw's deadly *sonic emitter* weapon.

T'Chaka was killed by **ULYSSES KLAUE** (a.k.a. Klaw,) an adventurer searching for Vibranium. As a young man, T'Challa swore to **AVENGE** his father. He spent the next several years **training** to be physically and mentally **worthy** of becoming the next Black Panther.

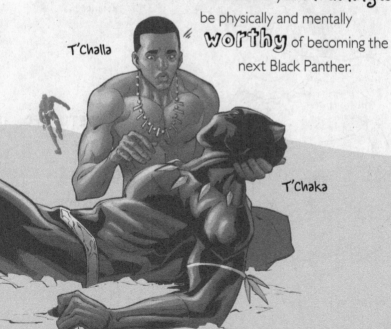

T'Challa

T'Chaka

T'Challa **traveled the world** and attended universities in **EUROPE** and the **UNITED STATES** so that he could learn about the modern world.

I've got degrees in mathematics, engineering, computer science ...

He eventually **RETURNED HOME** to face the **challenges** necessary to become **KING** and **BLACK PANTHER.**

Through **grueling** **PHYSICAL** and **MENTAL** trials that included having to **BEAT** the **best warriors** of the nation's other tribes, he was declared **worthy** by Bast. Hooray!

These trials can gather huge crowds. Equal parts danger and excitement!

T'Challa was **NOW** the **King of Wakanda.** He also took on the **MANTLE** of Black Panther and ingested the heart-shaped herb that bestowed **INCREDIBLE PHYSICAL POWERS** on him.

Tails up!

Don't forget the panther suit ...!

Ingesting the heart-shaped herb gives T'Challa impressive **Super-powers:**

The strength to wrestle a **charging rhino** to a stop—check. ✓

Must have done something to upset him ...

Greater speed and agility than any **Olympic gymnast**—check. ✓

Reflexes sharp enough to dodge a **BULLET**—check. ✓

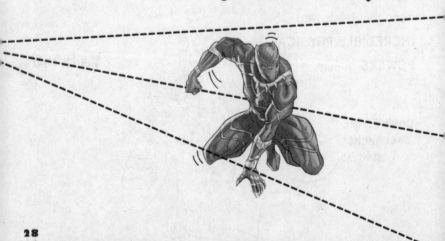

Enhanced stamina, allowing him to **RUN** and **FIGHT** for far longer than a normal human—check! ✓

squeak

SUPER-HUMANLY acute **hearing, taste, smell,** and **sight**—check, check, check, and CHECK! ✓ ✓ ✓ ✓

T'Challa can see **farther** and detect small details, such as a subtle scent, that would easily escape a normal human. This can have both pros and cons. (There are **some smells** that **NOBODY** wants to be able to smell!)

 He is also extremely (*extremely*) intelligent. You get the picture: T'Challa, with his super-powers, is awesome. Perhaps even

invincible ...

Panther claws

POW!

(Talk about making an entrance)

Sleek, all-black suit

Vibranium heels

If being an **ENHANCED** human blessed by a panther goddess wasn't enough, T'Challa has used Wakandan technology to create a **vibranium-laced battlesuit.** The Vibranium can absorb the kinetic energy of bullets, **explosions,** and super-human **kicks** and **punches.**

All of this means T'Challa remains unharmed as he continues to fight. On the battlefield, you'll find him out front, leading the way!

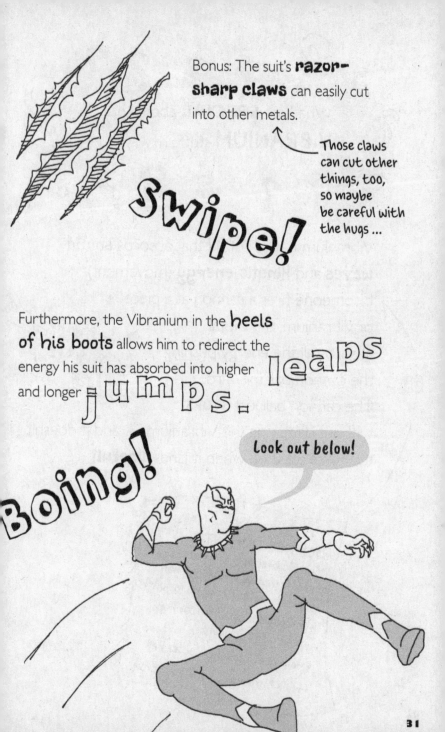

Bonus: The suit's **razor-sharp claws** can easily cut into other metals.

Those claws can cut other things, too, so maybe be careful with the hugs ...

swipe!

Furthermore, the Vibranium in the **heels of his boots** allows him to redirect the energy his suit has absorbed into higher and longer jumps. leaps

Boing!

Look out below!

What's so **SPECIAL** about this **VIBRANIUM** stuff anyway?

Vibranium is a 𝗺𝗲𝘁𝗮𝗹 that absorbs **sound waves** and **kinetic energy** (movement). If someone fires a cannon at a piece of Vibranium, the metal absorbs all the energy pushing the cannon ball forward. The cannon ball just **STOPS** without damaging the Vibranium ... and it doesn't even make a thud when it lands. **Useful!**

SCIENCE MOMENT:
Kinetic energy is the energy transferred to an object that makes it move. Examples include:
- Gunpowder causing a cannon ball to fire forward
- Your foot kicking a soccer ball
- Hulk throwing a tank at Ultron

CRACK!

Death rays? No problem! Mystical hammers? Pfft! They can't even dent this shield!

Captain America's **shield** is made out of a unique combination of Vibranium and other metals that no scientist has ever been able to reproduce (and many have tried!). It's thought to be one of the few **indestructible** objects on Earth!

The energy-absorbing properties of Vibranium make it extremely valuable for **scientific** and **military** uses. It has made Wakanda one of the RICHEST nations ON EARTH. Unfortunately, its high value means that **Super Villains** such as the Red Skull, Klaw, and many others are always trying to get their hands on it ... and they're not fussy about what methods they use! **(Stay tuned for more on this later ...)**

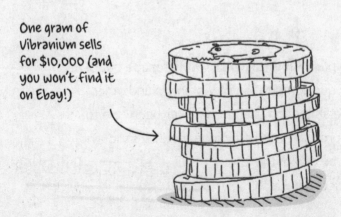

One gram of Vibranium sells for $10,000 (and you won't find it on Ebay!)

VIBRANIUM is a unique metal. However, it's not the only amazing one. Here are a few other metals that ANY Super Hero would be PROUD to own:

Anti-Metal: This RARE form of Vibranium is found only in the Antarctic. It **vibrates** in a way that causes the molecules of other metals near it to break down and sometimes even liquify!

Adamantium: This metal is difficult to create and keep in its liquid form. Once it hardens, it is totally INDESTRUCTIBLE.

Uru: Used by the Dwarves of Asgard, this metal is not only nearly indestructible but can also hold magic spells and enchantments. Hero Thor's **hammer** is made of Uru and it is enchanted to return to his hand whenever he calls it.

Carbonadium: Is a **flexible** but not-quite-as-indestructible version of Adamantium. It is also extremely poisonous!

Metal-wearing Avengers hero Iron Man is not a fan of Anti-Metal ... for obvious reasons.

Evil villain Ultron likes to make his robots out of Adamantium. No guesses as to why!

Wash your hands after touching this one!

Keeping it in the family

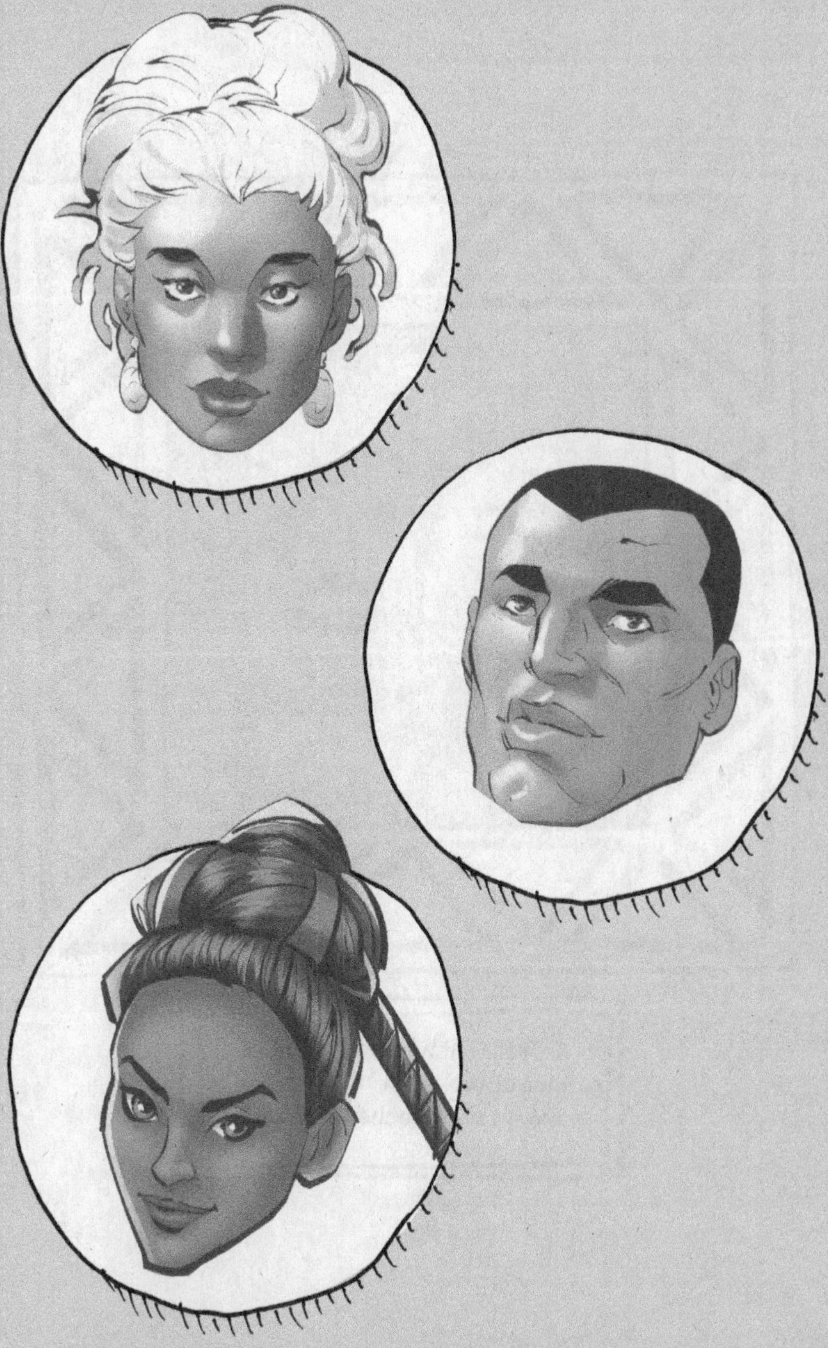

T'Challa with his father and
king of Wakanda, T'Chaka,
and his stepmother, Ramonda.

Wakanda's Royal Family

Despite his **formidable skills** and **powers,** T'Challa **cannot** rule all Wakanda **alone.** (Give the guy a break, huh?)

To **protect** his nation's borders and secrets as well as **maintain peace** between the tribes that make up Wakanda, T'Challa keeps a **vast network** of **friends, allies,** and **family** members in the Royal Household. His family are among his **GREATEST SUPPORTERS.**

WE ♡ U

T'Challa's real mother was a **doctor** and **scientist** named **N'Yami.** She died shortly after T'Challa was born. His father, T'Chaka, remarried to a woman named **Ramonda,** who raised T'Challa as if he was her own son. She also gave T'Challa a little sister named **Shuri.**

N'Yami

King T'Chaka

Queen Ramonda

Big Brother is watching me!

T'Challa

Princess Shuri

It's a family tree—get it?!

Queen Ramonda is fiercely loyal to T'Challa and to the nation of Wakanda. Since T'Chaka's death, she acts as an **advisor** to her son, and she is more than capable of **running the country** when his duties take him elsewhere*.

(***** Black Panther's duties have taken him all over Earth— and even into outer space!)

I talk. He listens.

Ramonda's **knowledge** of **ancient traditions** helps T'Challa balance his nation's old ways with his vision for a **technologically advanced** future.

Speaking of technology: ENTER **SHURI!**

Shuri is T'Challa's **super-tough** little sister.

Like her brother, she is both **smart** and **strong.**

She knows all about technological advances.

That's because she **INVENTS** them!

Leap like a
leopard and
punch like
a panther!

POW!

Shuri has **trained her whole life** to be a
fierce fighter. She always knew she would have to
take on the mantle of **Black Panther** if
anything should happen to her brother.

42

She **got her chance** when T'Challa was near death after being severely injured by the Super Villain **Doctor Doom.** (Don't worry, he recovered!)

We ♥ the heart-shaped herb

Er ... a little sugar, please?

Shuri **faced the trials** and ingested the **HEART-SHAPED HERB** that gives the drinker extra powers.

Morlun: dresses smart but can never check his own reflection.

THEN she successfully **helped defeat** an evil vampirelike villain named **Morlun,** who wanted to feed off the **mystical energy** that comes from the Black Panther's connection to powerful goddess **Bast.**

... Phew, that sounds like a busy introduction to the role of the Black Panther!

As if this wasn't enough, Shuri has also gained **supernatural abilities** through contact with the **SPIRITUAL REALMS** that are also part of Wakanda. Because of this:

She has the ability to form a **rock-hard skin** ...

Going up ...!

... and even **GROW** in physical size.

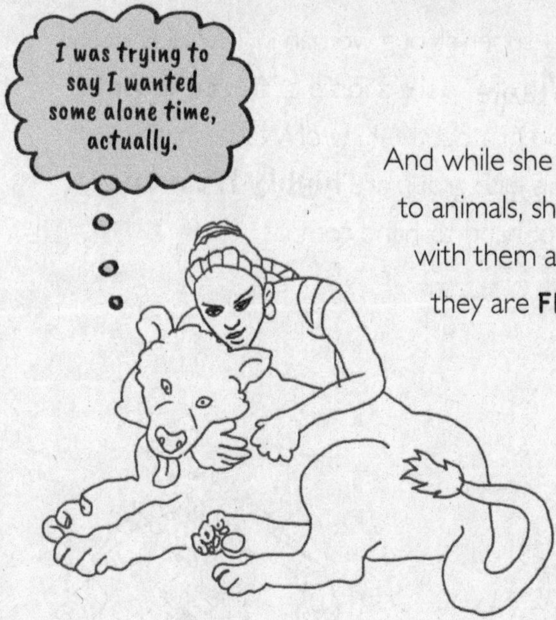
I was trying to say I wanted some alone time, actually.

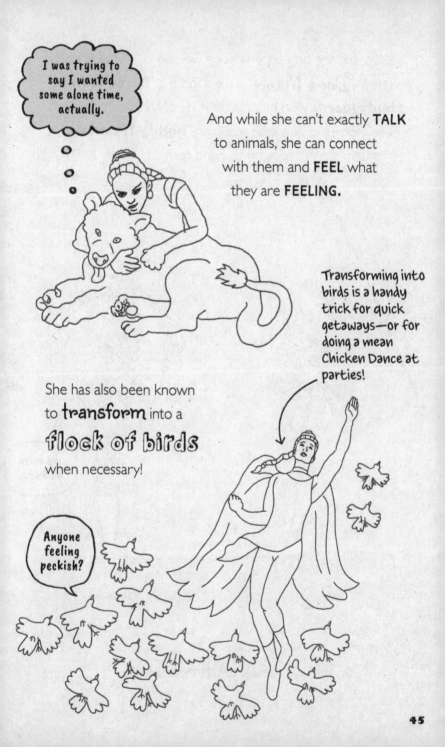

And while she can't exactly **TALK** to animals, she can connect with them and **FEEL** what they are **FEELING.**

Transforming into birds is a handy trick for quick getaways—or for doing a mean Chicken Dance at parties!

She has also been known to **transform** into a **flock of birds** when necessary!

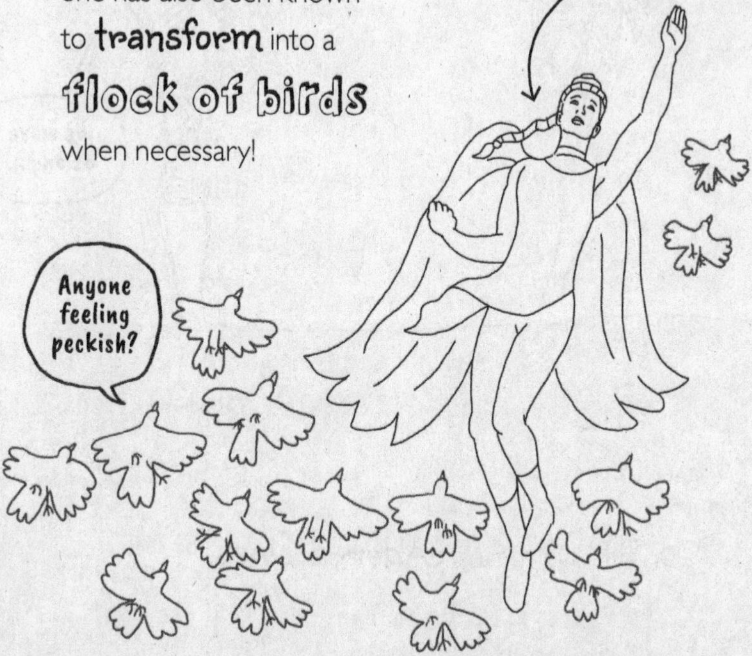
Anyone feeling peckish?

Shuri isn't the only super-strong woman in T'Challa's life. The **Dora Milaje** are a force of **fierce female bodyguards** who protect the King of Wakanda. The women of this elite group are **highly trained** in multiple styles of hand-to-hand combat.

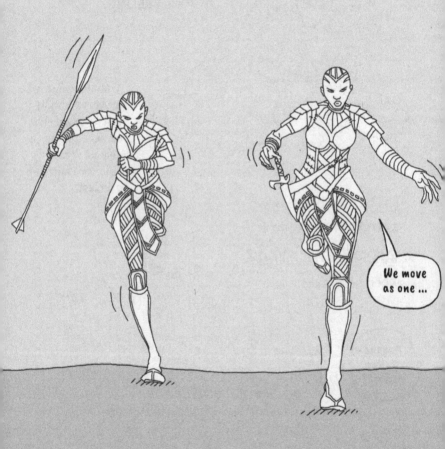

Dora Milaje means **"Adored Ones."**

They become **skilled** with **ancient weapons** such as **swords** and **spears,** as well as modern models featuring the latest Wakandan tech. Depending on the situation, they can **slip quietly through the shadows** or **fly into battle** at their king's side.

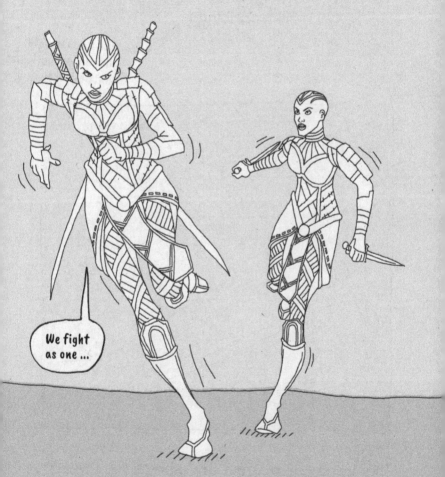

We fight as one ...

Their motto is: **"To serve, to fight, to be fierce, to be fearless."**

The **Dora Milaje's training** includes **combat** and **weapons,** but that's not all. They must **ALSO** become proficient in **other skills** that are **useful to their king.** They learn multiple **languages** and all manner of **science** and Wakandan **technology.**

And you thought your schoolwork was kind of demanding!

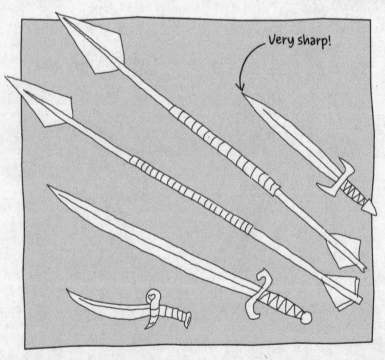

Very sharp!

They are ready to **protect and serve** their king and nation in **ANY** situation. Take a look at those fierce Vibranium spears, and you'll soon get the point!

As T'Challa attempts to slowly open Wakanda up to the **rest of the world,** the Dora Milaje have become well practiced in **the art of diplomacy and politics.** And where there's diplomacy and politics, there's also **spying** and **espionage!** The Dora Milaje keep their eyes on both their king's **enemies AND his allies.**

I'm glad they're on MY side!

OKOYE: one of the fiercest, one of the finest!

One of the **most talented** members of the Dora Milaje is named **Okoye.** She is also one of the **highest-ranking** members of this elite group.

Okoye has traveled with T'Challa on many of his adventures in the world outside Wakanda and **fought next to** some of the world's **other** great Super Heroes.

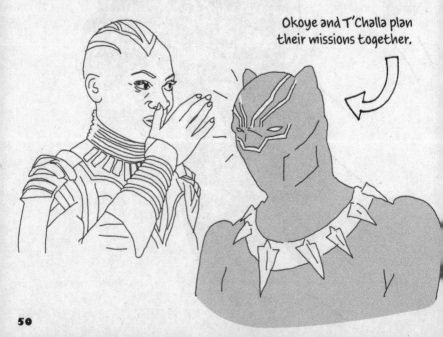

Okoye and T'Challa plan their missions together.

Others **close to the king** include **W'Kabi,**
T'Challa's second in command and the **CHIEF** of
Wakandan security. Much like Black Panther's
ally Winter Soldier, W'Kabi has a powerful
mechanical arm. Awesome! This loyal friend
sacrificed himself to save T'Challa and Shuri from
the energy **vampire Morlun.** (Him again.)

W'Kabi

Next up: **N'Gassi** and T'Challa's **Uncle S'yan***. Both have been trusted advisors to T'Challa over the years, helping him make the **best decisions possible.** And both men have sometimes acted as the **KING** when T'Challa was not available.

*Uncle S'yan was even a Black Panther once. He ruled Wakanda while his nephew was too young to be king!

Towering over all T'Challa's advisors is one considered to be one of the **MIGHTIEST WARRIORS IN WAKANDA:** a **GIANT** of a man named **ZURI,** who was a companion of T'Challa's. He fought next to his king in **many battles** and was friends with many of T'Challa's Super Hero allies.

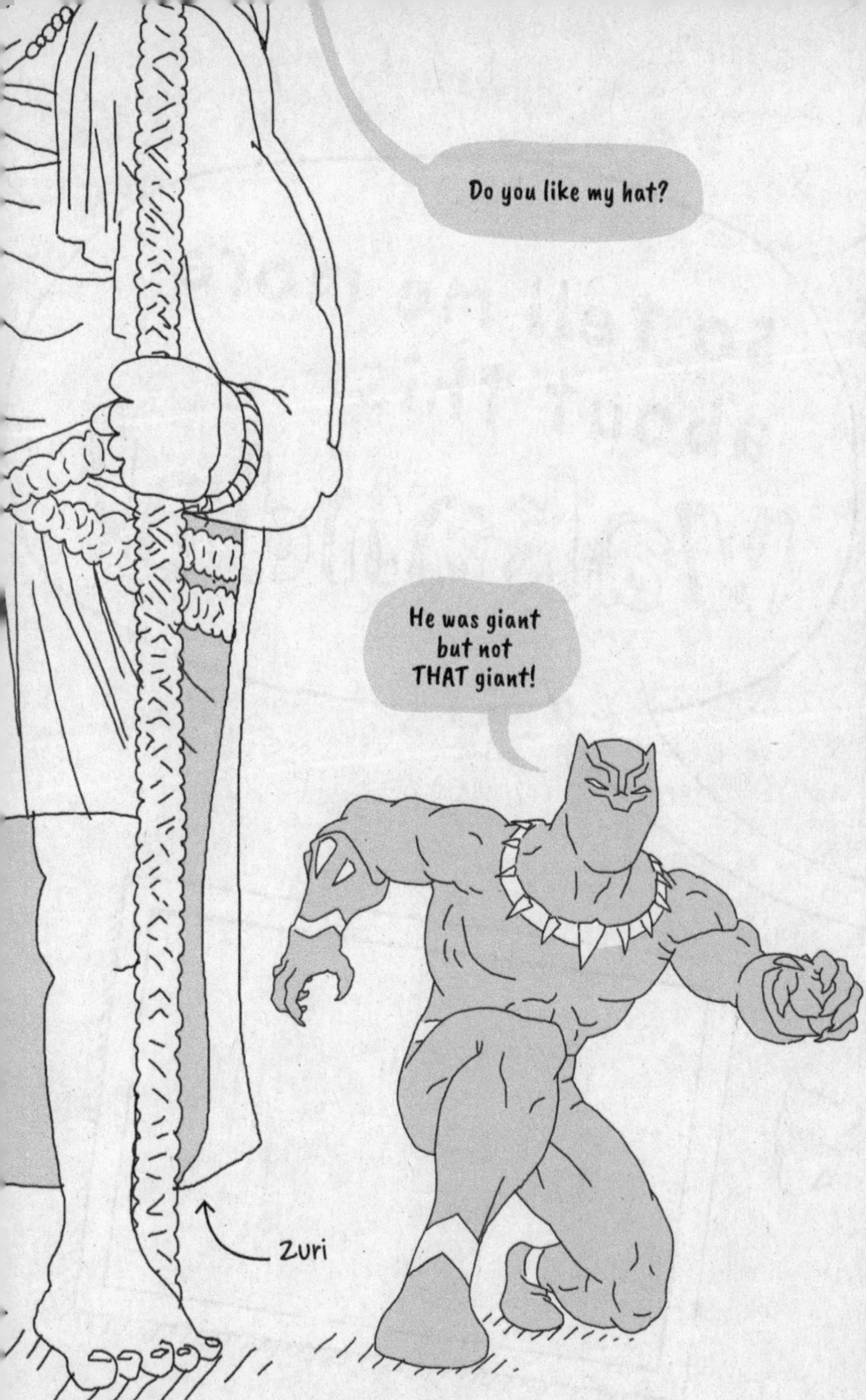
Do you like my hat?
He was giant but not THAT giant!
Zuri

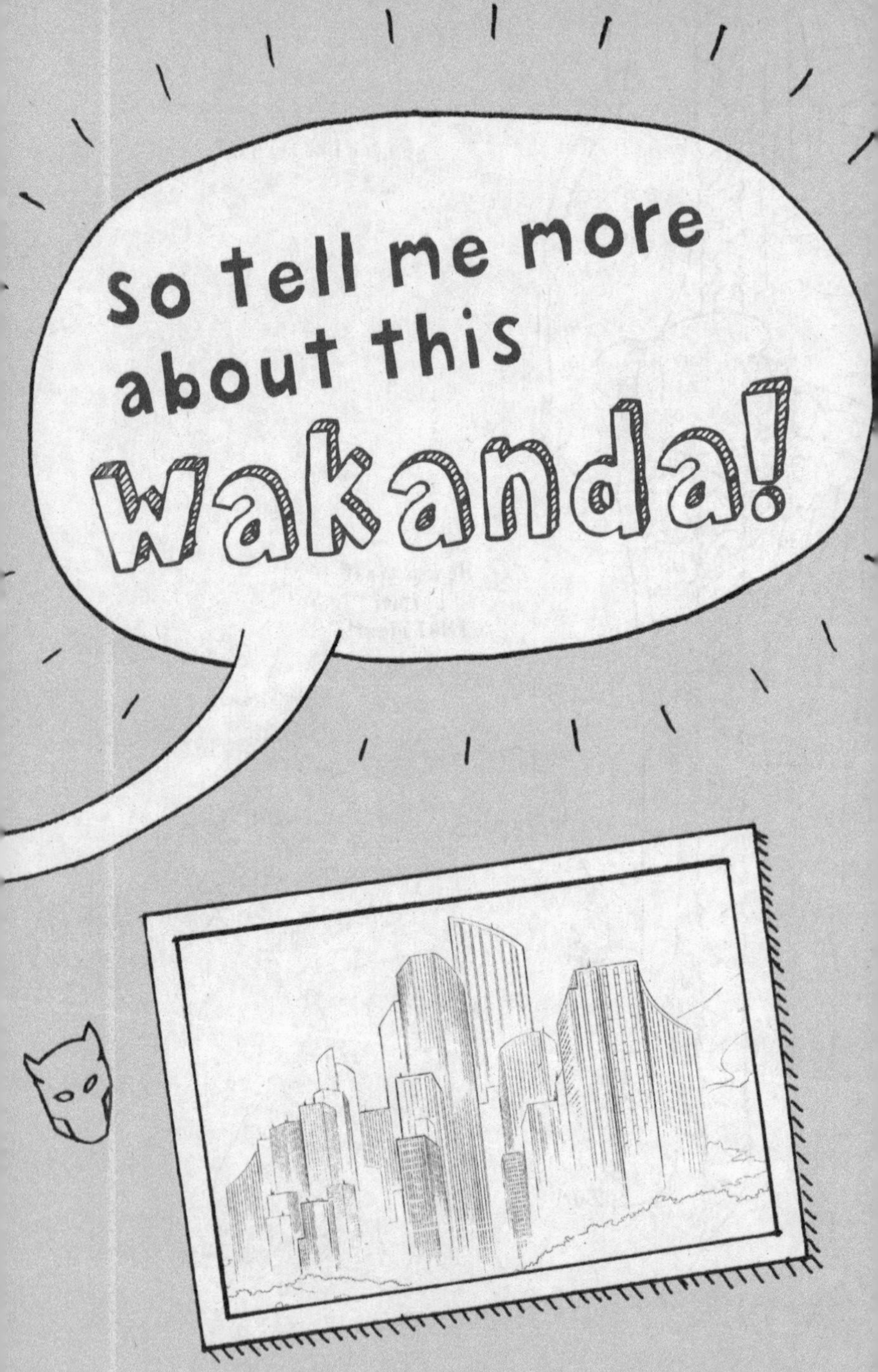
So tell me more about this Wakanda!

Wakanda Forever!

WE ♡ WAKANDA

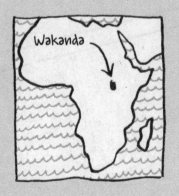

Wakanda

Wakanda is located in **Eastern Africa.**
Many natural features, including **mountain ranges,
dense swamps,** and **jungles,** have made it
difficult to reach for outsiders.

Until the **modern age** of **planes** and **helicopters,**
these natural features helped Wakanda's rulers keep
their nation's secrets **hidden** from the prying eyes
of the world. **SECRETS,** you say? **WHAT SECRETS?**

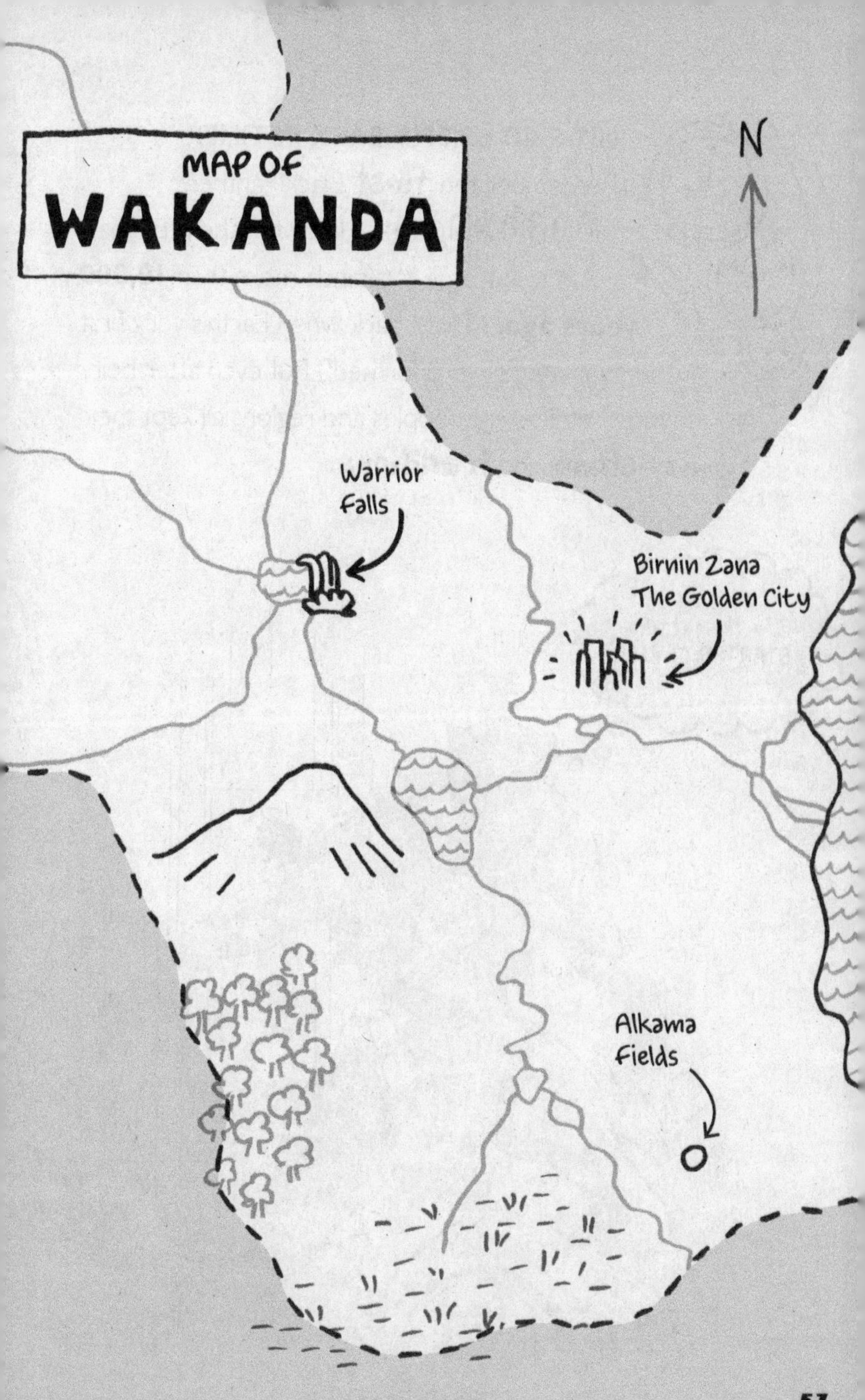
MAP OF
WAKANDA
N
Warrior Falls
Birnin Zana
The Golden City
Alkama Fields

LET'S GO BRIEFLY BACK IN TIME: Remember the **first** Black Panther, **Bashenga?** He united the area that was to become Wakanda more than **10,000 years ago.** (That's back when Earth's very first human nations were formed!) But even after being united, the different peoples and regions all kept their own **customs** and **traditions.**

I'm the cat who **STARTED IT ALL!**

Bashenga

NOWADAYS, Wakanda still has many different tribes. They include the **Jabari Tribe,** who worship the **ape god, Ghekre.** Some of the tribes remain loyal to their own gods and goddesses, but since the time of Bashenga, it's **the Panther Goddess, Bast,** who has dominated the region. Panthers rule, okay?!

Did you know that Wakanda is full of **powerful supernatural forces***, all **restless** and **hungry** for **power?** The other deities and their human followers are constantly looking for ways to overthrow Bast and her champion:

the Black Panther!

* You would think that supernatural beings would have better things to do!

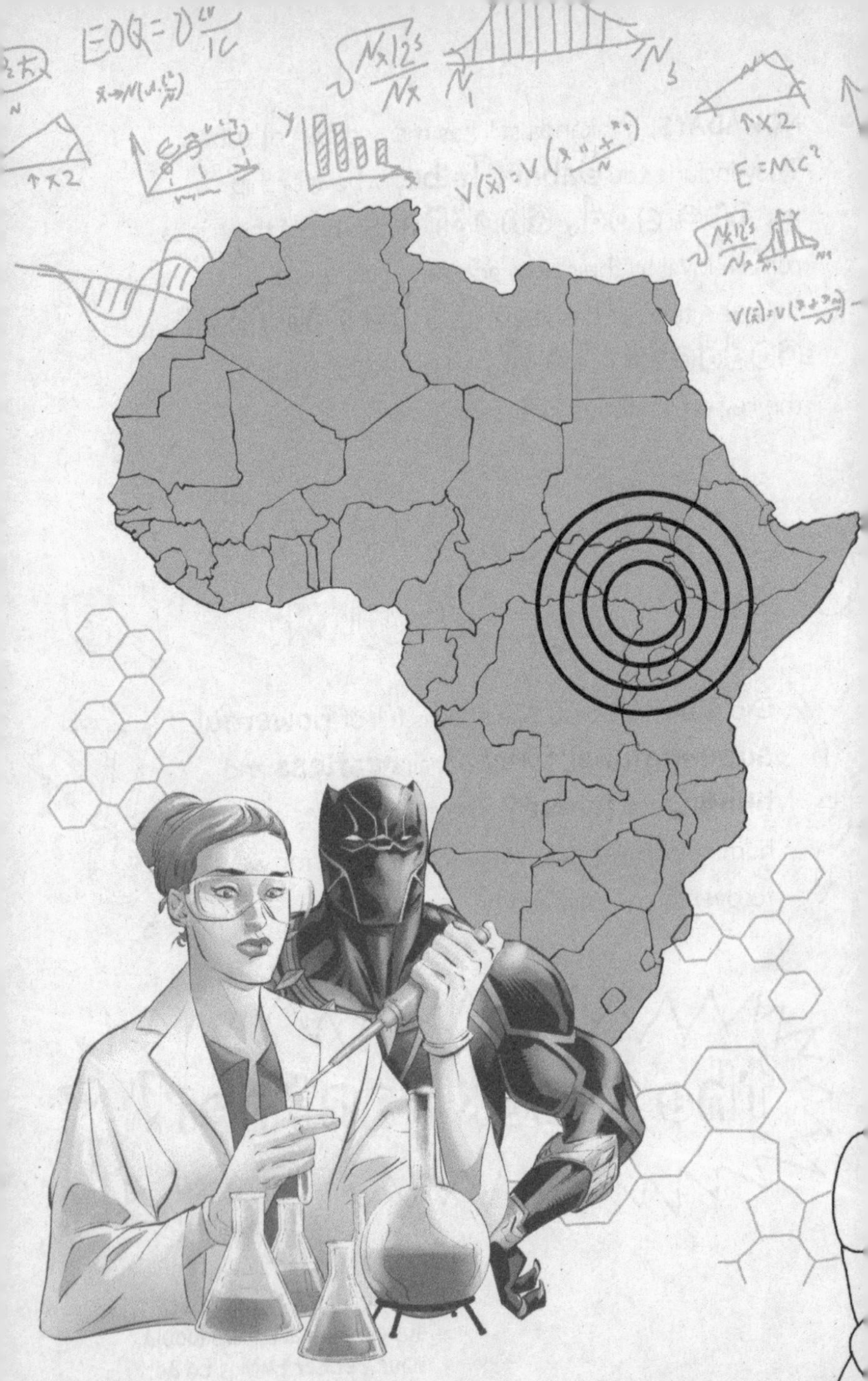
E = Mc²
↑×2

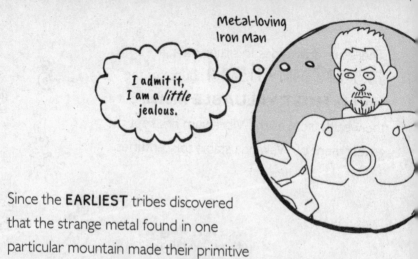

Metal-loving
Iron Man

I admit it, I am a little jealous.

Since the **EARLIEST** tribes discovered that the strange metal found in one particular mountain made their primitive **spears** and **knives** and **shields** more POWERFUL, Vibranium has spurred Wakandan technology forward. ▷▷▷ Without the world knowing it, this small African nation has become one of the **wealthiest** and most technologically **advanced** countries on the planet.

(Shh!)

In more recent times, T'Challa has expanded Wakanda's expertise in almost **EVERY** field of **science** on Earth, including **medicine, aviation,** and **energy production.** Even geniuses like Tony Stark (a.k.a. **IRON MAN**) and the Super Villain **DOCTOR DOOM** are a little jealous.

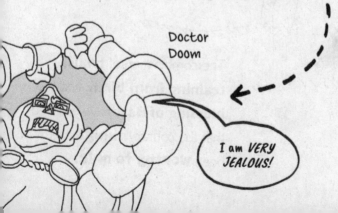

Doctor
Doom

I am VERY JEALOUS!

There are downsides to sitting on a **mountain-sized** source of the **world's MOST VALUABLE metal,** but the wealth from all the Vibranium has kept the government of Wakanda stable for centuries.

Er ... move along there ... nothing to see here ...

Mountain-sized source of Vibranium

VIBRANIUM

The combination of **trials, training from birth,** and the **blessing of Bast** have ensured that the country's **kings** have been **worthy to rule.**

Back through the royal family tree, almost **EVERY king** of **Wakanda** has been a descendant of:

You can trust Black Panther to keep ALL your secrets (and plan your surprise parties!)

BASHENGA.

And they have all recognized the importance of keeping their country's most valuable resource a secret. For **hundreds of years,** they have been **successful,** but that has started to **change** ...

Think **YOU** can keep a secret? So did Wakanda—until it became clear that some outsiders had learned the **SECRET** about Vibranium. Boo! Wakanda had to **repel** several attacks from these forces, including one from Red Skull, a villain who was working with the Nazis during World War II.

Over time, the attacks **grew** more frequent, putting the people of Wakanda in ever more danger. T'Challa decided that with so much at stake, he couldn't continue to allow authority to rest in the hands of **ONE** person. (Even if that one person was the Black Panther!)

As a result, T'Challa has slowly **changed** the way that Wakanda is **ruled.** The current setup is known as a

CONSTITUTIONAL MONARCHY

which means that if something happened to either T'Challa or Shuri, law (or a government) would rule the land. This would provide **more stability** than the old method of choosing a leader: trials by combat. T'Challa also opened the country up to the rest of the world, meaning its location on the map is no longer secret.

(The Vibranium cat has been let out of the bag ...)

This was the

vibranium meteorite

that made Wakanda **extremely wealthy** ...
but this **WEALTH** comes with a downside. (That's
right—money isn't everything, kids!) Vibranium has
magical properties that have plunged the nation
into **supernatural turmoil.** *Yeesh.* And
this supply of magical metal has also made the no-longer-
secret Wakanda the **TARGET** of every country and **SUPER
VILLAIN in the world. Hold onto your hats** ...

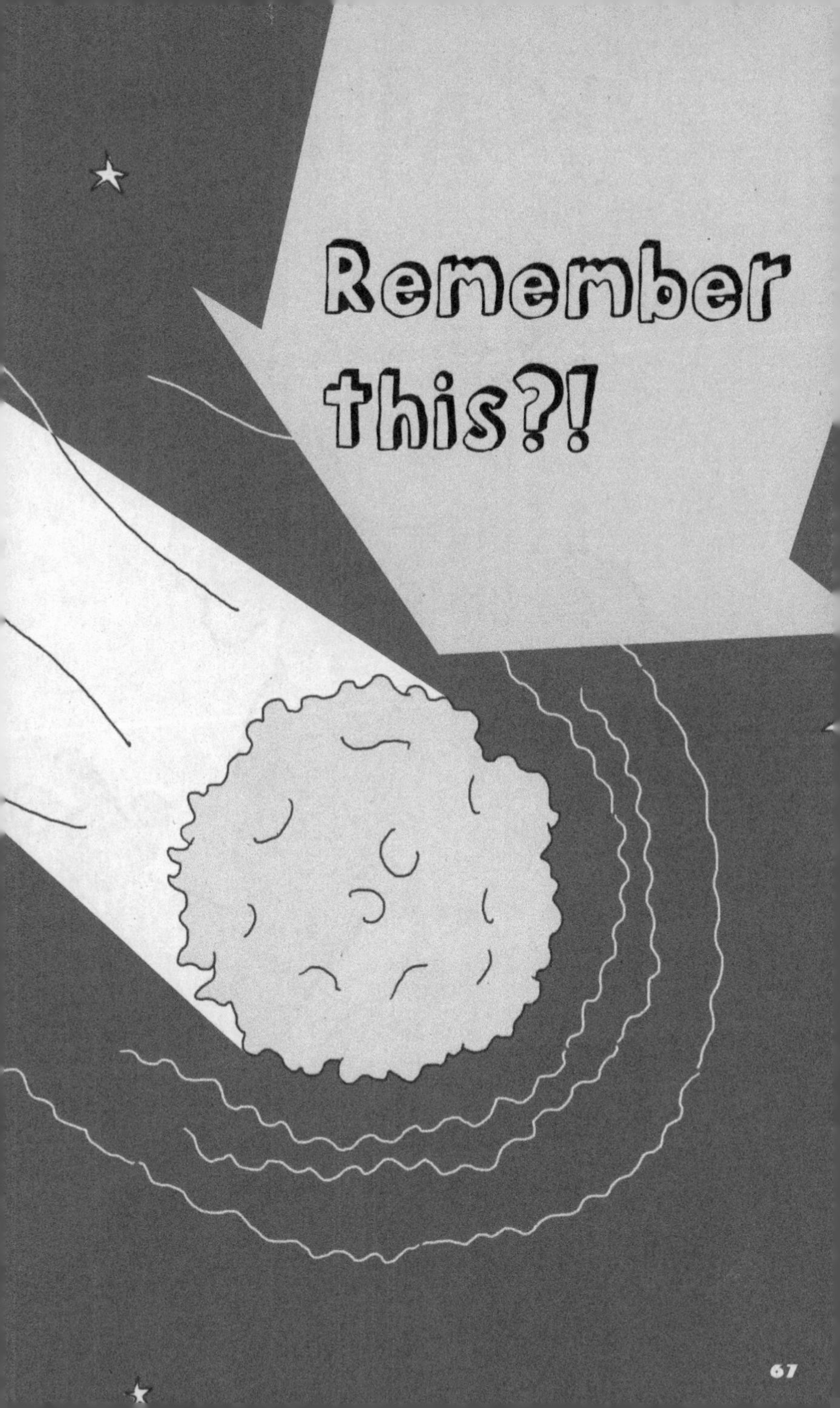
Remember this?!

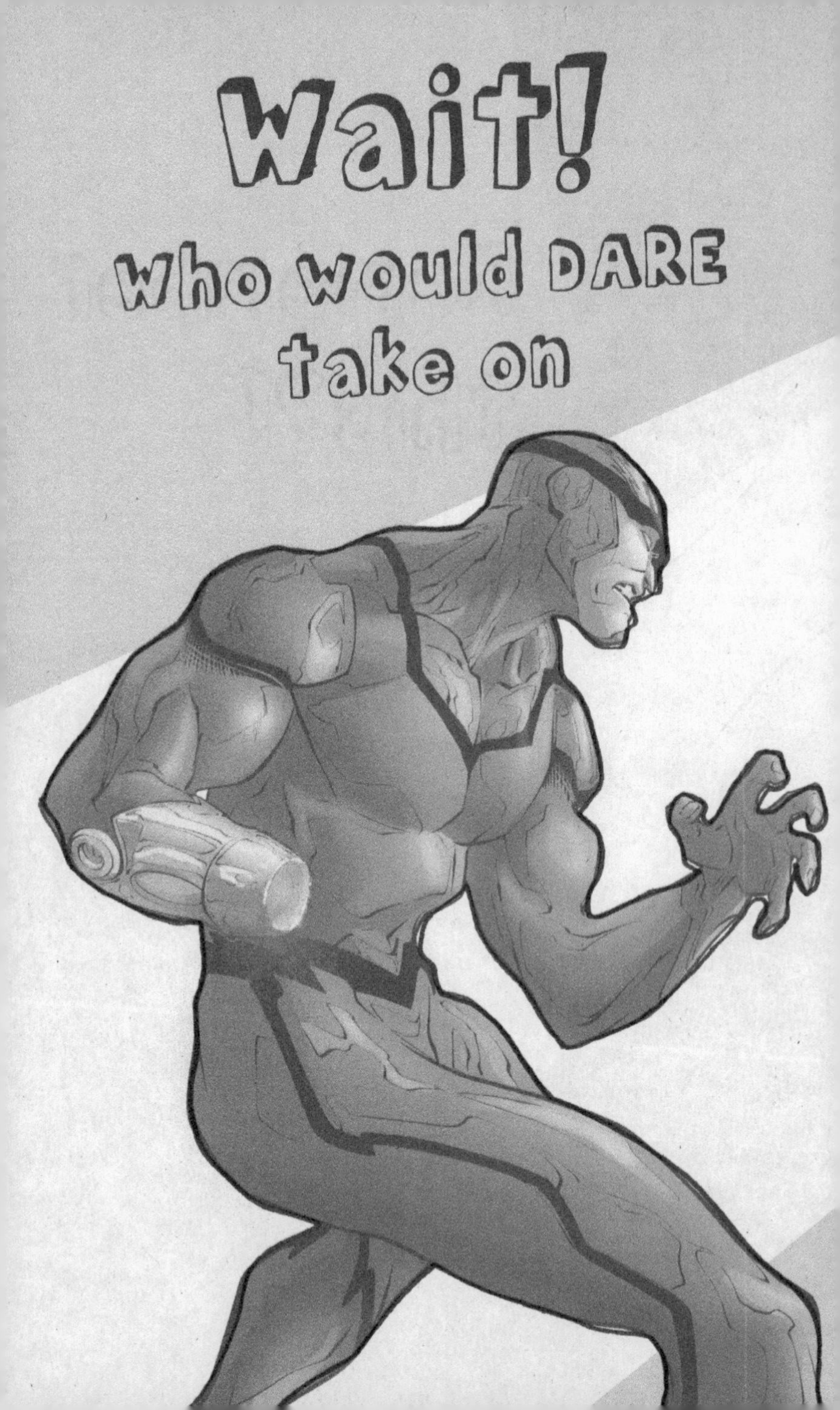
Wait!
Who would DARE
take on

the Black Panther?!

RED SKULL

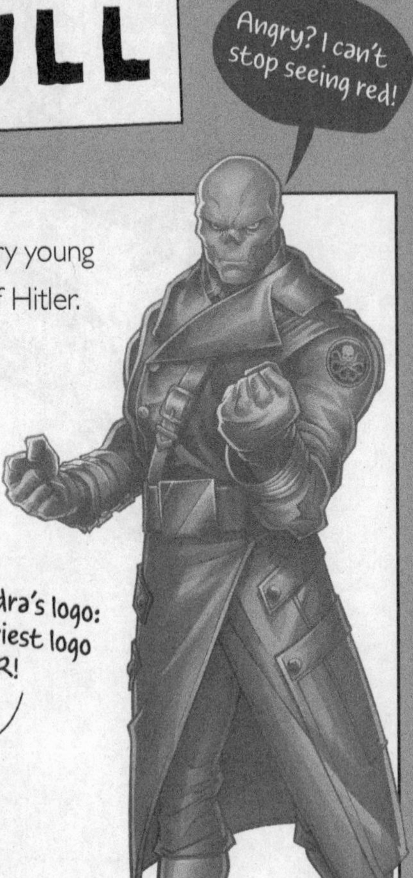
Angry? I can't stop seeing red!

Johann Schmidt was an angry young man taken in by Nazi leader Adolf Hitler. He was personally trained to be a ruthless spy and later became leader of world-domination-seeking **Hydra.**

Hydra's logo: scariest logo EVER!

Eventually, Schmidt took a version of the **Super-Soldier Serum** that turned Steve Rogers into CAPTAIN AMERICA.

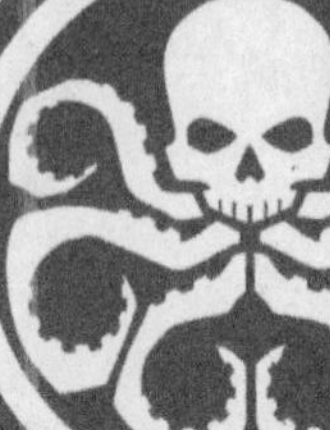
SSS

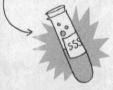

But where the serum brought out the **BEST** in Steve Rogers, it brought horrible physical changes to Schmidt, turning him **bright red!** Now, more than ever, **DOMINATION** and **CONQUEST** were this **twisted, evil military genius's** only goals. **Not exactly** ideal.

As the leader of Hydra, the Red Skull has fought with **more than one** Black Panther over the decades and with the Avengers. The Red Skull has even **ESCAPED DEATH** time and time again—often with the aid of Nazi scientist **Arnim Zola,** who once transferred the Red Skull's evil consciousness into **clones** of his body. Double the trouble!

Hi kids!

YOU'RE the clone!

No, YOU'RE the clone!

KLAUE

Some people will do anything to get their hands on Vibranium, like young scientist and adventurer **ULYSSES KLAUE,** who needed it for one of his **INVENTIONS**.

Klaue hired a group of **mercenaries** to help him sneak into Wakanda to **steal** some Vibranium. Not a smart move! A **fight** ensued. Klaue killed T'Chaka, who died saving his son's life, and Klaue did not even get the Vibranium. At least this event gave young T'Challa the resolve to become the next Black Panther.

BOOOOM!

During another attempt to acquire
Vibranium, one of Klaue's inventions
accidentally turned him into a being of

pure sonic energy!))))

Sounds disastrous? Not really. It made Klaue
a big shot in the world of villains and one of Black Panther's
deadliest foes, taking the name **Klaw.** Now, with a
sound converter mounted on his wrist, he can emit sonic
blasts capable of shattering steel. And if he is harmed, his
body just **reforms.**

Killmonger by name ...

ERIK KILLMONGER

Before he got his scary, very **OBVIOUSLY VILLAINOUS** name, Killmonger had the Wakandan name **N'Jadaka.** When he was young, he was kidnapped by some renegade Wakandans. He grew up on the run with his captors. After finally killing them, he ended up in **New York,** but by then he was *ANGRY* and *BITTER.* Maybe even a little *TWISTED.*

When T'Challa began to open Wakanda up to the world, N'Jadaka returned **home.** He was accepted as a **lost son** of **Wakanda,** but he secretly wanted to sit on the throne himself. Or maybe to see his homeland **destroyed*.**

*His childhold may have left him slightly conflicted ...

Killmonger has **fought** Black Panther several times over the years. And no matter how many times he is defeated, he returns again and again with **PLOTS** to **bring down** his mighty home nation of Wakanda. He is extremely strong, though not super-human, and extremely intelligent. He sometimes employs items such as a **Vibranium-tipped spear** and **Vibranium armor:**

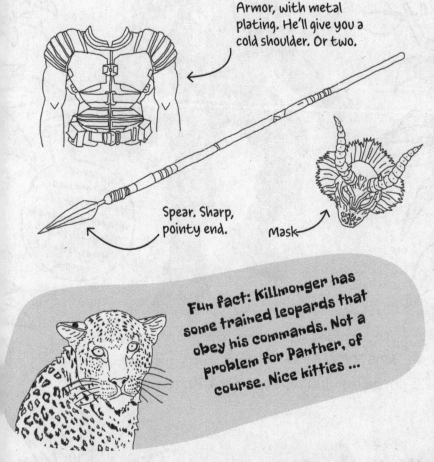

Armor, with metal plating. He'll give you a cold shoulder. Or two.

Spear. Sharp, pointy end.

Mask

Fun fact: Killmonger has some trained leopards that obey his commands. Not a problem for Panther, of course. Nice kitties ...

KRAVEN THE HUNTER

Kraven has to ingest a little of his potion now and then to maintain its effect. Let's hope it doesn't taste like sprouts!

Sergei Kravinoff is a former member of the **RUSSIAN ARISTOCRACY** who became a big game hunter in Africa more than 100 years ago. Yes, **100,** you read that right …

At some point in his **early** career, Kraven was given an **herbal** concoction that not only enhanced his physical abilities, but also **slowed** his aging. Even though he is ⓞⓥⓔⓡ ⓐ ⓒⓔⓝⓣⓤⓡⓨ ⓞⓛⓓ, he still looks like a young man.

Much like Black Panther's, Kraven's **SPEED, REFLEXES,** and **SENSES** are greatly heightened.

Whoo, this guy is FAST ...

He can run **as fast as a cheetah,** and he can find his prey with a combination of his **tracking skills** and **super-sharp senses.**

His strength is super-human, allowing him to lift over **2 tons!** That's approximately two cars, or one rhino.

The computer program that eventually became known as

ULTRON

was originally an **AI (Artificial Intelligence)**
developed to **help** humanity. Instead, it became
sentient, with **thoughts** and **feelings** of
its own. Unfortunately, it thought humans were
not worth helping and felt they
might be better off being
exterminated! YIKES!

Ultron has **clashed** with
the Avengers, including Black
Panther. It would
love a shiny new
Vibranium body,
so its glowing red
eyes are always
focused on
Wakanda.

ᒐᒐᒐᒐᒐ

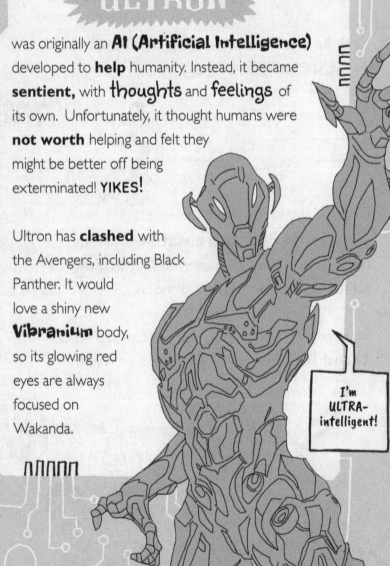

I'm
ULTRA-
intelligent!

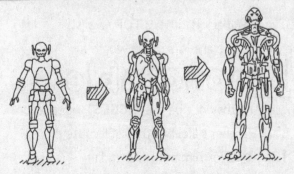

Ultron has had several robot bodies. Nothing to do with fashion—it's just that each time it is defeated, it comes back with a **new** and **deadlier** body. It usually makes them out of **ADAMANTIUM,** but a **VIBRANIUM** body would make it truly indestructible. And truly happy. And truly lethal.

As a ₵𝕆₥ℙᵁₜ𝔼ℝ ℙℝ𝕆𝔾ℝ₳₥, Ultron can slip away through any computer or the internet whenever its body gets destroyed or its plans defeated.

Where did he go?

Heh! Heh!

⚠ VIRUS DETECTED

Ultron is like the computer virus you can never get rid of. He comes back again and again and again ... and again and ...

You've met Black Panther's **TOP** (worst) foes, but there are lots more worth a **dishonorable** mention. These guys may not be the **BIGGEST** nuisance in Black Panther's life, but they still cause plenty of **trouble** for him and Wakanda:

Achebe: a wicked, mystical warrior.

DOOOOOM!

Doctor Doom: an evil genius with skills in science and the mystic arts.

Don't say he didn't warn you about the doom.

Malice: a mutated former member of the Dora Milaje. Bad news. (The clue is in her name!)

M'BAKU: a super-strong adversary who wants the Wakandan throne.

Arnim Zola: an evil Hydra scientist (another one!) who uploaded his brain into a computer and became a robot.

Zola's not exactly Black Panther's foe, but he's a close buddy of Red Skull. Enough said!

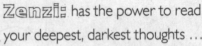

Morlun: a mystical-energy vampire. He sucks.

Zenzi: has the power to read your deepest, darkest thoughts …

LUCKILY, Black Panther has plenty of friends to help him battle these foes and keep Wakanda safe. Turn the page to find out more …!

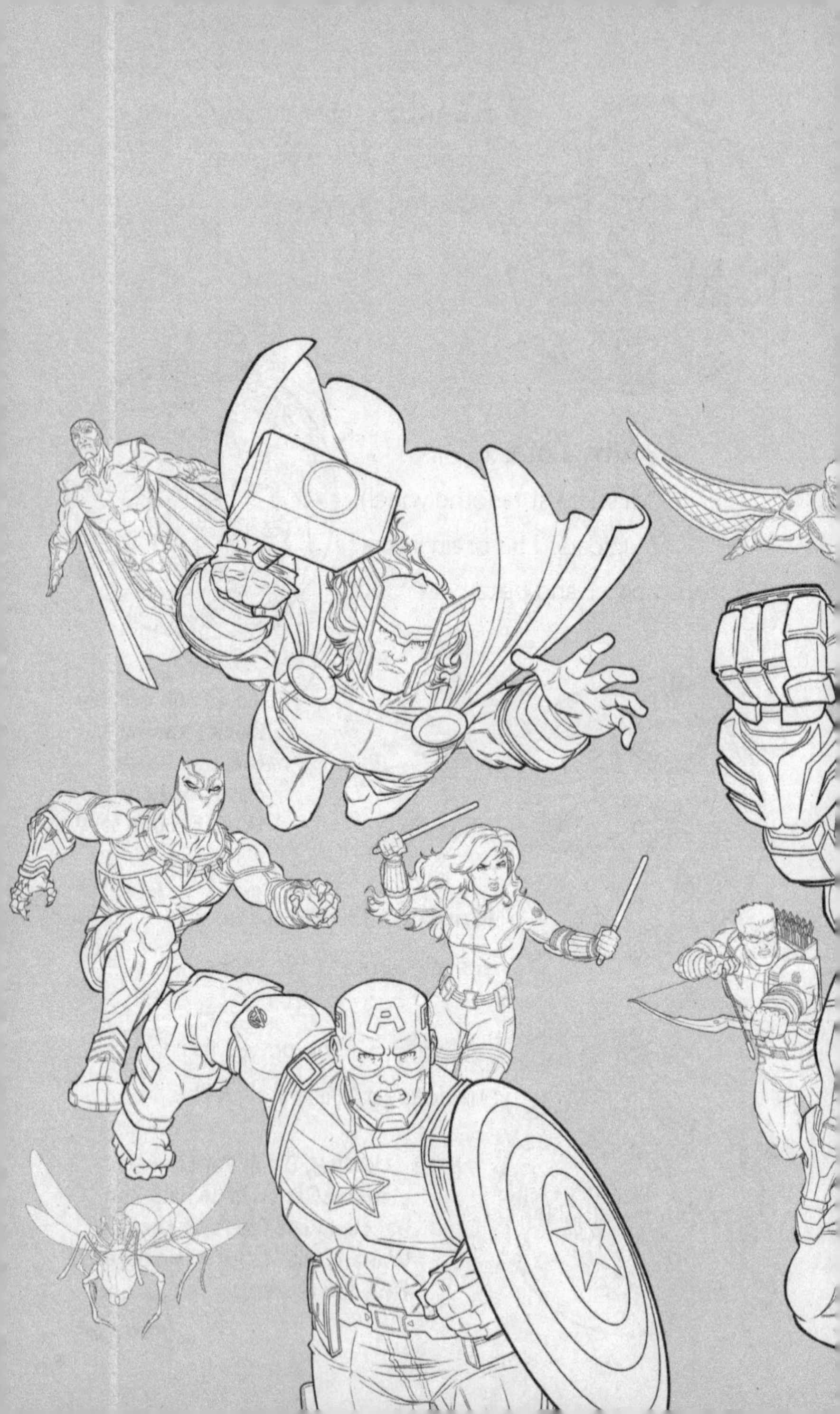

Allies and Avengers to the rescue

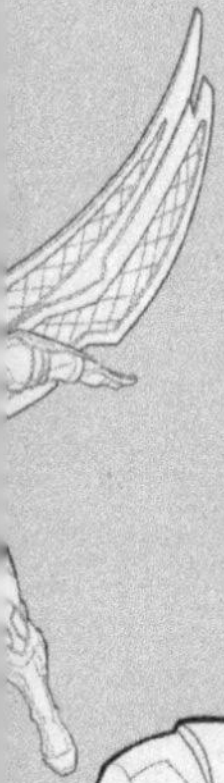

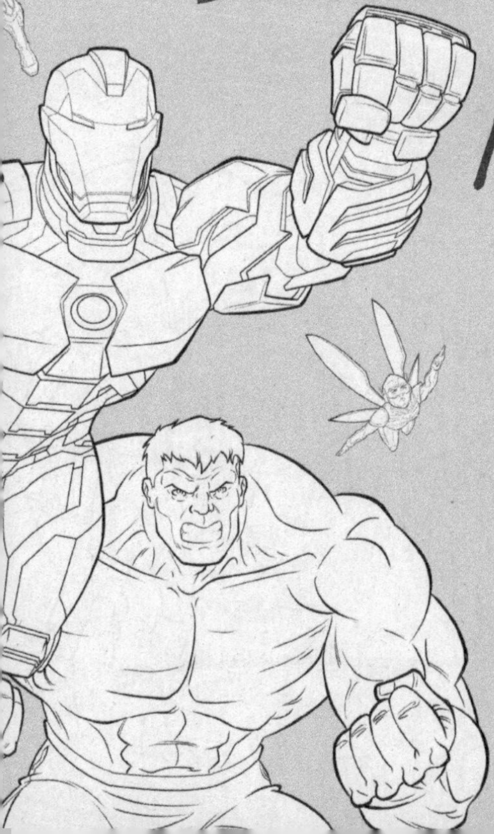

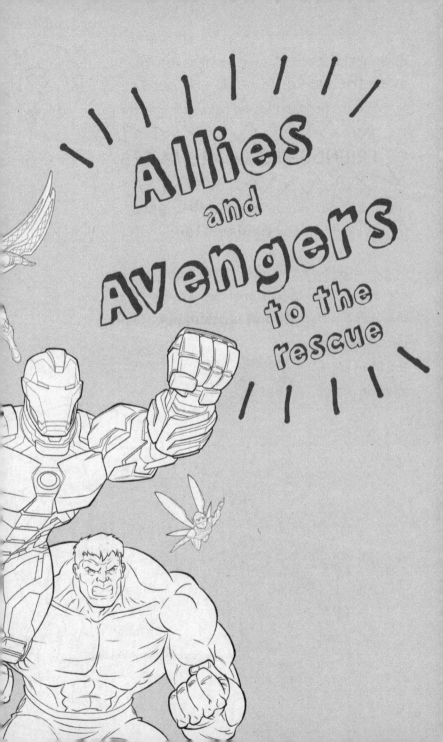

Black Panther's adventures have taken him **all over the world.** Thankfully, while he's come up against many fiendish foes, he has also forged many

FRIENDSHIPS AND ALLIANCES

with everyone from the **Mighty Avengers** to your friendly neighborhood **Spider-Man.**

The Avengers are one tricky team to be a part of. Sometimes you're in, sometimes you're out. In a team like this, **strong leadership** is important. Luckily, everyone on the team knows who's in charge.

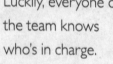

I'm in charge.

Black Panther has been a **member of the Avengers in the past.** Though the responsibilities of being a king have pulled T'Challa back to Wakanda, he will always remain an **ALLY** to them all.

Usually the Avengers **band together** under the leadership of Captain America and Iron Man. But even the **best** of friends sometimes fight—especially *Captain America* and *Iron Man.* When this happens, the heroes all have to pick **sides.** As an experienced king, Black Panther does his best to be **DIPLOMATIC** on these occasions. Guys, guys …

At the top of the Avengers roster:

Captain America,

often known as **CAP***. Once sickly young Steve Rogers, Cap was brought to the peak of human perfection by a combination of a secret **SUPER-SOLDIER SERUM** and mysterious vita-rays. Super!

* It's faster for his friends to shout in a fight!

Captain America formed a **lasting friendship** with the nation of Wakanda when he helped the Black Panther named **Azzuri** repel an invasion by the villainous Red Skull and Hydra.

Suspended animation: a.k.a. sleeping for a realllly long time.

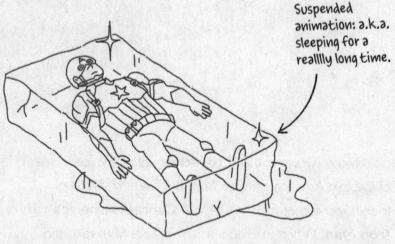

An accident once put Cap in **SUSPENDED ANIMATION** for decades. Now awake and back in action, this living legend is friends with Azzuri's **grandson,** T'Challa. Yes, Cap's that old.

Captain America and Black Panther have very similar physical powers. They are both considered to be **peak human.** Their *strength, speed, and endurance* are at the highest levels of human ability. They also both have enhanced **reflexes, agility, and senses.**

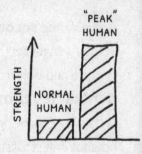

Cap has said that the Black Panther's ability to tap into **supernatural forces** (SPOOKY!) would give T'Challa an edge if they ever had a fight. It hasn't happened yet. Maybe if a game of chess got out of hand?

Arguably the **second most important** figure in the Avengers is this man here: TONY STARK— the one and only Iron Man. Like T'Challa, he has a **genius-level intellect** and a **talent** for **inventing** technology. Stark began his career as a hotshot industrialist, but after cobbling together a **ROBOTIC SUIT OF ARMOR,** he became something more— **a Super Hero!** And a rather shiny one, too.

Shiny

Stark refined the suit with sophisticated AI computers, repulsor rays, and jet boots, and presto …

IRON MAN

was born!

Shiny

Very shiny

Iron Man was a **founding member** of the Avengers, and as another **PROTECTOR** of **THE WORLD,** he has fought Super Villains side by side with Black Panther. He and T'Challa use science and technology to make the world **a better place.**

Others have worn the Iron Man suit, but let's face it— it's a better fit on Tony Stark.

You thought we got supernatural before, but that's about to get **even stranger** when we meet

Doctor Strange!

My diagnosis? Evil Eye strain!

Doctor Stephen Strange was not always the **Sorcerer Supreme.** He was once a gifted **surgeon.** But then a car accident left his hands crushed beyond the repair of normal medical science.

Desperate for a cure, he sought out a **LEGENDARY TEACHER** of mystical knowledge known as the 𝔸𝕟𝕔𝕚𝕖𝕟𝕥 𝕆𝕟𝕖. The Ancient One taught Doctor Strange the mystic arts. Then, when he passed on to a higher dimension, Strange took his place as protector of the Earth from the dark magics and things that **LURK** just beyond reality. Ugh! Wish you hadn't looked?

As both defenders of the world and keepers of **mystical secrets,** Black Panther and Doctor Strange often have reason to **CONSULT** with each other and work together.

From tech and magic to **arachnids** and all things webby: Meet T'Challa's friend, New York teenager Peter Parker. He gained amazing super-powers when he was bitten by a **radioactive spider.**

Peter's powers include super-human strength, lightning-fast reflexes, and a **spider-sense** that warns him of imminent danger. Peter can also climb walls like a spider, and his agility and sense of balance are far beyond those of even the best Olympic gymnast.

A tragedy made him realize that he had to use his powers **FOR GOOD,** and then ... ta-da—

Peter Parker became **Spider-Man!**

Though he usually sticks close to home*, he sometimes teams up with Black Panther when the Wakandan visits NYC.

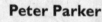

*That's why they call him the Friendly Neighborhood Spider-Man!

Say the villain Kraven unleashed **cheetahs** on New York. Spidey could trust that if **BIG CATS** were involved, he could call on the biggest cat of all, **Black Panther.** You don't need Spidey senses to tell you that they'd work well together!

Time for selfies when things are all wrapped up!

Cheetahs in New York is odd enough, but the Black Panther has teamed up with Spider-Man for some even **wilder** and **weirder** adventures—such as fighting

Stegron the Dinosaur Man.

You are getting big and green and lizardy ...

Don't stare into his eyes: Stegron used hypnotic powers to turn humans into prehistoric creatures.

This strange 𝕝𝕚𝕫𝕒𝕣𝕕-𝕝𝕠𝕧𝕚𝕟𝕘 scientist was trying to take over the world with

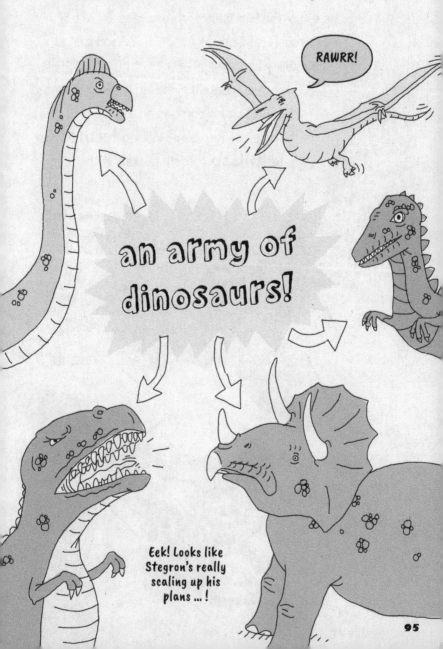

Panthers, spiders ... what next? **BIRDS**, of course! When the Red Skull kidnapped Sam Wilson, he subjected him to strange energies as part of a plot to defeat Captain America. Wilson gained the ability to **communicate with birds** by telepathy and took a falcon named **REDWING** as his companion. But instead of helping the Red Skull, Wilson **teamed up with Cap** to defeat him. Ouch!

Clearly destined to be a high flier in the Super Hero world!

Black Panther later used Wakandan technology to arm Wilson (a.k.a. Falcon) with a high-tech battlesuit and a **harness** with **wings.** This allowed Sam to fly **HIGHER** and **faster.** And as with his *own* suit, Black Panther put a weave of Vibranium into the Falcon's suit to provide resistance to physical damage such as gunfire and **punches** from super-strong foes. **Awesome!**

People say cats and birds don't mix. Try telling that to the Falcon and Black Panther! Sam has shown himself to be a **TRUE HERO** as both a member of the Avengers and on his own, and a **great friend** in times of need.

Here's a friend who sometimes looks like a foe:

the Hulk!

Like T'Challa, **Bruce Banner**—the man behind this
big, green monster—is a genius-level
scientist. But instead of a dose of heart-shaped herb,
Banner took a dose of **radiation** while saving a
young boy from the explosion of a gamma bomb.
The bomb was Banner's own invention.
Whoops!

SMASH!

Er ... smash
what? I'm out
of here ...

Bruce Banner is a key
part of the Avengers.
He is useful in a crisis.
But don't make him
angry. He might end
up a little smashy.

The radiation **mutated** Banner into a savage, green-skinned monster known as the Hulk. As the Hulk, his strength has **NO LIMITS**—the **madder** he gets, the **stronger** he gets! He's also close to indestructible and heals instantly from any wounds that he does get.

Hulk and Black Panther have occasionally **fought.** You wouldn't want to be in the way when that happens. Oh dear, no! But despite Hulk's **rage** and **MONSTROUS** nature, he and Black Panther have mostly been allies.* Which is best for anyone nearby as well as for them!

*Better keep letting Hulk have the last cookie, Black Panther.

Bruce Banner is **one Hulk,** but there have been other versions of the big, green hero who have been less ... er ... friendly. T'Challa has created a massive Vibranium armored suit called the **Wakandan Hulkbuster** for the times when he has to go **toe-to-toe** with larger-than-average foes—such as Amadeus Cho's Hulk.

Meow!

You're not seeing double: Amadeus Cho shares the same big, green powers as Bruce Banner's Hulk.

This Hulkbuster is shaped like a GIANT KITTEN! Maybe people should try distracting Black Panther with a ball of yarn ...

If **Black Panther** is your **buddy,** you'll probably get up close to his Vibranium and Wakandan technology at some point. He's cool about sharing it to help his **flying friends** (Falcon) and **ANGRY friends** (Hulk!) alike ...

Vibranium makes **EVERYTHING** work better. Almost all of Wakanda's technology benefits from the metal's properties. This can only be good for Black Panther—and his friends:

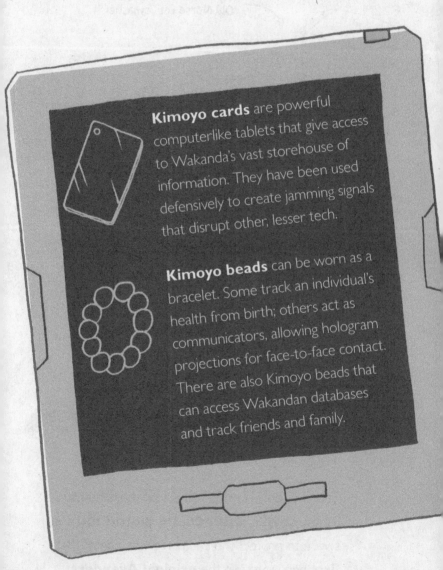

Kimoyo cards are powerful computerlike tablets that give access to Wakanda's vast storehouse of information. They have been used defensively to create jamming signals that disrupt other, lesser tech.

Kimoyo beads can be worn as a bracelet. Some track an individual's health from birth; others act as communicators, allowing hologram projections for face-to-face contact. There are also Kimoyo beads that can access Wakandan databases and track friends and family.

Who needs Black Panther's Vibranium when you have your own weapon made of a magical metal?

Mjolnir (Me-ol-near)—
Old Norse for "smasher"!

Virtually immortal,

Thor is the son

of Odin, the king of a land called **Asgard.** He is super strong, an incredible fighter, and **almost** indestructible.

These gifts made Thor **STUBBORN, VAIN,** and **ARROGANT** (bet you would have been, too), so Odin sent him to Earth as a mortal.

Thor not only learned to be a bit more humble, he also came to **appreciate humanity** and swore to protect the Earth. He was one of the **first** heroes to join the **original Avengers.**

A hammer may seem old fashioned, but it's as efficient as Black Panther's tech at getting the job done.

Don't even try stealing my thunder!

Thor's weapon is an **ENCHANTED HAMMER** called Mjolnir, with which he controls **storms** and **lightning**. He hurls Mjolnir with devastating power and it always returns to his hand. (Just don't call it a hammerang!)

Time to head to space with marvelous

Captain Marvel!

Carol Danvers was an ace US Air Force pilot who was recruited by **S.H.I.E.L.D.*** as a spy. But on a mission in space, Carol was bombarded by energy from an alien device. It turned her into one of the **MOST POWERFUL** heroes from Earth—ever. And everyone marveled!

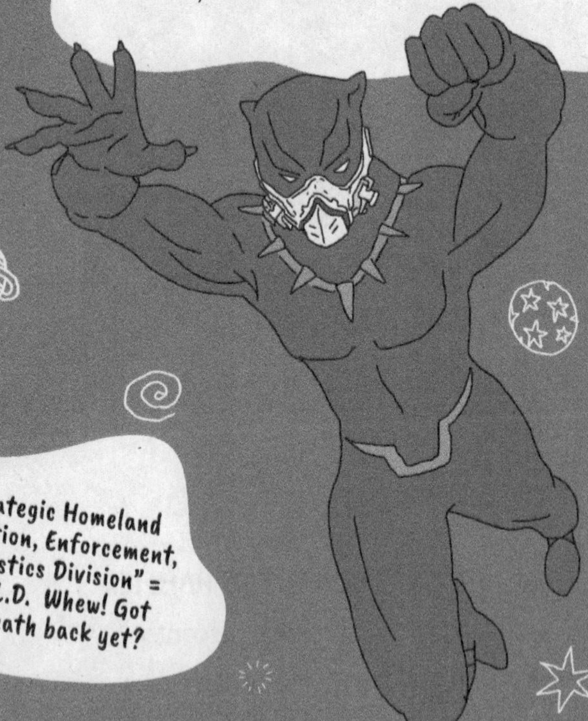

* "Strategic Homeland Intervention, Enforcement, and Logistics Division" = S.H.I.E.L.D. Whew! Got your breath back yet?

She is super strong and resilient to physical attack, and can also **fly** at super speed—even in cold, airless outer space. She can also project powerful blasts of energy capable of **smashing** through the thick hulls of intergalactic battleships.

PS: Carol has a cat named Chewie, who is really an alien being from another universe.

Carol and Black Panther joined a team of **cosmic heroes** who specialized in risky space missions. **Lift off!** (And then home to feed the cat.)

From one of the **STRONGEST** to the smallest:

Ant-Man!

There's no job too small for him to handle.

He also has a helmet that lets him issue commands to ants. It's extremely helpful at picnics.

Scott Lang was **NO HERO.** Let's be blunt: he was a **thief.** Until the day he stole a high-tech suit belonging to **inventor** and sometime hero known as Ant-Man **Dr. Hank Pym.** Dr. Pym could see that the young thief had the **potential** to be something more. He allowed Lang to keep the suit, and a new Ant-Man was born. Or maybe hatched. As a Super Hero, Lang soon proved himself **worthy** to be an Avenger!

By using the  Pym Particles contained in the suit,

Just call me "larger than life!"

Lang can shrink to the size of ant or grow to **giant stature.** At ant size, he retains his human-sized strength. And he has **SUPER STRENGTH** in his **GIANT FORM.** You could say he's a small wonder *and* a big deal!

By combining his thievery skills with his **shrinking powers,** Ant-Man can sneak into any place with ease. He helps Black Panther investigate a puzzling crime **deep underground,** and has also worked with Hank Pym—the original Ant-Man.

Are we nearly there?

(Sigh) Not yet.

Hi there!

Like her **counterpart** Ant-Man, Janet Van Dyne also wears a high-tech battlesuit that makes use of the Pym Particles. She is the Super Hero known as

THE WASP!

She can **shrink** to the size of a wasp and fly at incredible speed with a pair of insectlike wings.

She retains her human-size **strength** even when small, meaning that she can **LIFT** any object or take out any villain that she could at full size.

Zzzap!

But when she really wants to pack a punch, she can discharge powerful bolts of electricity that she calls her wasp stings.

When Black Panther **FIRST** met the Avengers,
he **rescued** the Wasp and her teammates from
the clutches of the villainous Grim Reaper.

In gratitude, T'Challa was swiftly made a member of

Earth's
Mightiest
Heroes.

That's the Avengers,
by the way. Every
team needs a
catchphrase.

Are you afraid of spiders? Think they bite? Well, you're right! **The Black Widow** wears **bracelets** called **widow bites** that emit high-voltage shocks to her foes. (Let's hope that's not you.) And even they are *nothing* compared to the Black Widow herself.

A black widow spider is one of the most dangerous spiders in the world ... it can kill with one bite. See where she got her name from?

Natasha Romanoff was raised to be a **SUPER-SPY** and master of **MARTIAL ARTS.** But when she spied an opportunity to make the world a better place, she didn't hesitate. She **switched sides** to join the agency S.H.I.E.L.D., and eventually became a member of the Avengers.

Besides being an expert in martial arts and other forms of **hand-to-hand combat,** Black Widow is an Olympic-level athlete and gymnast. It pays to be flexible.

POW!

As part of the Avengers, Black Widow and Black Panther needed all their strength and abilities to defeat the awesome cosmic villain known as **THE COLLECTOR.** This fiend had decided the Avengers would be the ultimate prize in his collection. **Yikes!**

Hmmm ... What shall I collect next?

He collects objects. Powerful objects, magical objects. And sometimes people ...

C'mon, can you lend us some arrows?

Here's a guy who never misses a trick. Or a target.

Clint Barton, a.k.a. **Hawkeye,** was born with an amazing sense of **aim.** He trained with **the bow and arrow** from an early age, becoming one of the **greatest marksmen IN THE WORLD.** Unfortunately, Clint initially set his sights on a criminal career. Tut tut!

Clint crossed paths with the Avengers while trying to **STEAL** tech from Tony Stark (Iron Man). Inspired by the **heroic deeds** of Iron Man and Captain America, he decided to change his aim and use his skills for good. No more thieving! He later became an Avenger, too.

(It's surprising how many Avengers used to be thieves.

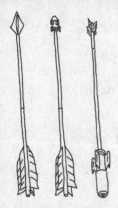

Hawkeye is **a great athlete** and hand-to-hand combatant. **UNLIKE** Black Panther, he has no enhanced abilities ... but he does have enhanced arrows! His quiver is full of **trick arrows** that contain explosives, smoke bombs, nets, cables, tracking devices, and more. He's a hot shot alright!

A pizza-delivery arrow would be useful!

Go fetch!

Remember the villain **Ultron?**

This android, named **Vision**, was **CREATED BY** Ultron.

Vision was meant to be part of **a trap** for the Avengers. But something went wrong with his programming, and he turned out to be **more human** than intended. Vision **turned on** Ultron and helped the heroes defeat him, leaving Ultron ultra unhappy!

Remember, kids ... be nice to your smartphones (in case they turn on you!)

Despite his **computerlike mind,** super strength, and ability to go from diamond hard to completely **intangible*,** Vision is one of the most human of the Avengers.

*This means he can walk through walls. Neat!

Um ... he's not really what I envisioned!

Ultron

Vision is now a great **ally of Black Panther** in the battle to stop Ultron getting hold of **VIBRANIUM.** You have to feel sorry for his rueful robot creator. (What ... not even a little?)

AS WELL AS being an *Avenger,* Black Panther has taken part in many **other** Super Hero team-ups from **ALL OVER** the place. Let's join him for some of his top tales:

1 The Black Panther has teamed up with the **Fantastic Four** (there are four of them and they're fantastic) many times over the years. So that's the Fantastic Five, then.

T'Challa has a special ally in their stretchy leader, **Mr. Fantastic.** He's one of the smartest men on the planet.

Both scientists, they have worked together to repel **alien** invasions, **extradimensional** invasions, and in fact **ANY SORT OF INVASION** that needed **brains** rather than **brawn** to quash it. Black Panther was even an official member of the Fantastic Four for a while. Panthertastic!

2

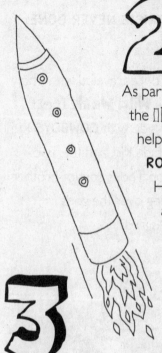

As part of a group of smart people called the Illuminati, Black Panther helped to put an out-of-control Hulk on a **ROCKET** and send him **into space.** Hulk launch! He was meant to land on an uninhabited planet where he could do no harm. But the Hulk came back. And he was angry. **Very, very** angry.

3

When T'Challa was wounded by Doctor Doom, Storm came whirling in to assist her old friend. As Wakanda's doctors battled to save T'Challa's life, the weather-controlling leader of the **X-MEN** fought to save his soul. Her opponent? None other than Morlun, the ever-hungry energy vampire.

What does a vampire have to do to get some nutrition around here?

... No time for a break! **A HERO'S WORK IS NEVER DONE.**

4

Black Panther once traveled with Thor to the old-time **Wild West.** They fought side-by-side with **COWBOYS** Kid Colt, the Rawhide Kid, and the Two-Gun Kid to stop Thor's sort-of-brother Loki from taking over the gods' homeworld, Asgard.

Yeehaw, we look pretty cool in these hats!

5 More recently, T'Challa stopped an alien **SKRULL** invasion of Earth. He then put together one of the strangest teams yet, to deal with threats beyond the scope of even the Avengers and S.H.I.E.L.D.— **The Agents of Wakanda.**

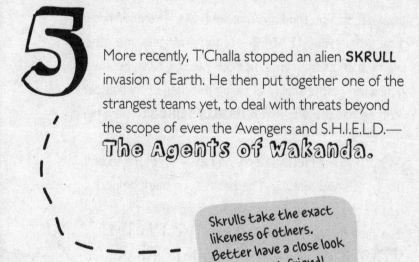

Skrulls take the exact likeness of others. Better have a close look at your best friend!

Team members serve as information gatherers and spies in the wider world. The star-studded line-up includes Okoye, Wasp, Man-Wolf, and a rather large martial arts expert named Fat Cobra. They've battled **the Void** (one of the darkest and most powerful beings in the galaxy), fought various vampires*, and had to deal with Prince Namor, the sometimes hero, sometime villain ruler of the underwater world Atlantis.

*NOT Morlun for once!

Void

So what do you think? We've seen Black Panther has been a member—and **LEADER**—of the Avengers and other teams such as the Fantastic Four. As T'Challa, he always bears the responsibility of being the King of Wakanda. And he has shown what it **really takes** to be a hero.

As both a king **AND** a hero, he has been there to help his friends and allies, and he has in turn been helped by them. It's not super-powers and advanced tech that save the day. Instead, it's their **bravery, friendship,** and **teamwork** that can withstand any trial or any villainy.

As the world and the universe get **WEIRDER** and **MORE DANGEROUS,** Black Panther and his friends will be there to protect Wakanda and all the people of Earth.

WAKANDA FOREVER!

Not everybody can say they've fought vampires and traveled into outer space and other dimensions. And with a totally cool suit ... and super-powers ... and a hover bike. Don't forget the hover bike.

Do you think you have what it takes?!

121

Glossary

Acute
Something that is heightened above and beyond a usual level.

Adversary
An opponent, or an enemy. Someone who might fight against you.

Ally
A friend, or someone who fights alongside someone else.

Android
A robot created to look like a human, with humanlike features.

Aristocracy
The highest class in some societies; often a position of power, wealth, and respect.

Asgard
Another-dimensional world, home to a godlike race of beings, including thunder god Thor.

Avengers
A squad of Super Heroes united to defend Earth from attacks no hero could face alone.

AVENGERS UNITE!

Clone
A genetically identical copy of a living thing, created in a lab.

Diplomatic
Capable of dealing with difficult situations often involving rulers, without taking sides, and able to reach a peaceful conclusion.

Dora Milaje
Wakanda's all-female, highly trained security force.

Enhanced
Made better.

Espionage
The practice of using spies to learn about other countries.

Hologram
A three-dimensional image, often projected from a holo-projector or computer.

Hull
The main body of a ship (whether in space or on water).

Hydra
An ancient, evil organization seeking worldwide domination and constantly reforming itself with new recruits.

Illuminati   Sounds mysterious!
A secret group of Super Heroes from different groups, with different skills, all working together behind the scenes.

Industrialist
A person in charge of running a company—or industry.

Ingest
To take food or drink into the body by swallowing it or absorbing it.

yum!

Invincible
Cannot be defeated or overpowered.

Mercenary
A person, often a soldier, who will fight for whoever will pay them.

Meteorite
A piece of rock that falls to Earth without burning up.

Mjolnir
A mighty, enchanted hammer that can only be wielded by those it deems worthy.

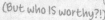

(But who IS worthy?!)

Mutation
A change to the DNA of a living thing, causing physical changes and differences and sometimes creating whole new species.

Norse
Ancient or medieval Scandinavian.

Peak human
Someone possessing heightened strength, speed, and reflexes compared to a regular human. Considered the best of the best.

Radiation
A discharge of energy, dangerous in large amounts.

Renegade
Someone who abandons their original team, country, or organization, switching to support the opposite side.

Top Secret!

S.H.I.E.L.D.
"Strategic Homeland Intervention, Enforcement, and Logistics Division"—a secret defense organization created to protect Earth from global threats.

Skrull
Alien species capable of shapeshifting.

Super-soldier serum
A formula, developed for US soldiers, giving those injected with it enhanced physical and athletic abilities.

Supernatural
Something existing outside scientific understanding, which is often hard to explain.

Tribe
A group of people joined together with one leader.

Unrelenting
Constant, never stopping.

X-Men
A team of mutants united together to fight for good under the leadership of genius Professor X.

Index

Achebe, wicked mystical warrior 80

Adamantium, a totally indestructible metal 35, 79

Agents of Wakanda 119

Ancient One, the legendary teacher of the mystic arts 91

Ant-Man, teeny-tiny super hero 12, 106–107

armored war rhinos (oomph!) 17

Asgard, Thor's homeworld 35, 102, 118

Avengers: the Earth's Mightiest Heroes 9, 12–13, 84–85, 109
    clashes with enemies 71, 78
    mighty members of 89, 97, 102, 106, 111, 112, 115

Azzuri, a former Black Panther 24, 86

Banner, Bruce a.k.a. the Hulk 98, 99, 100

Barton, Clint a.k.a. Hawkeye 112

Bashenga, the first ever Black Panther 19, 20, 58, 63

Bast, powerful panther goddess 20, 22, 27, 43, 59, 62

battlesuits, a Super Hero perk
    Ant-Man's 106–107
    Black Panther's 14–15, 30–31, 42
    Iron Man's 88, 89
    Falcon's 97
    Wakandan Hulkbuster 100
    Wasp's 108

Black Widow, assassin-turned-Super Hero 13, 110–111

brains, uploaded into robots 81

Captain America, the first Avenger 13, 24, 70, 85, 86–87, 96
    his indestructible shield 24, 33, 87

Captain Marvel, Super Hero powered by alien energy 104–105

Collector, the cosmic villain 111

Danvers, Carol a.k.a. Captain Marvel 104–105

dinosaurs (yes, really, dinosaurs) 94, 95

Doctor Doom (his name says it all) 43, 61, 80, 117

Doctor Strange, mystical super hero 90–91

Dora Milaje, fierce female bodyguards 46–49, 50, 80

dragon fliers 17

Falcon, Super Hero high-flier 13, 96–97

Fantastic Four, or five including the Black Panther 116, 120

Hawkeye, the greatest marksman 12, 112–113

heart-shaped herb (giver of powers) 22–3, 27, 28, 43

Hulk, the 12, 98–9, 100, 117

Hydra criminal organization 71, 86 and world domination 70

Illuminati, super-smart people 117

Iron Man 12, 35, 85, 88–89

Killmonger, Wakandan rival 10, 74–75

Klaue, Ulysses (villainous scientist a.k.a. Klaw) 25, 72–73

Kraven the Hunter 76–77, 93

Lang, Scott a.k.a. Ant-Man 106

Malice, former Dora Milaje 80

M'Baku, super-strong villain 81

Mjolnir (Thor's enchanted Hammer) 35, 102, 103

Morlun, vampire villain 43, 51, 81, 117

Mr. Fantastic 116

mutated creatures animals warped by Vibranium 20, 21

N'Gassi, trusted advisor 52

N'Yami, T'Challa's mother 40

Okoye, one of the fiercest and finest 50, 51, 119

Parker, Peter a.k.a. Spider-Man 92

Pym, Hank, the original Ant-Man 106, 107

Pym Particles 107, 108

Ramonda, Queen of Wakanda 38, 40, 41

Index continued

Red Skull villainous Nazi 24, 70–71, 96
   watch out, Wakanda! 64, 86

Rogers, Steve a.k.a. Captain America 70,
   71, 86

Romanoff, Natasha a.k.a. Black Widow
   111

Royal Talon Fighters 16, 17

S.H.I.E.L.D. Strategic Homeland
   Intervention, Enforcement, and
   Logistics Division 104, 111, 119

Schmidt, Johann a.k.a. Red Skull 70, 71

Shuri, T'Challa's super-tough sister 40,
   42–45

Skrulls (shape-shifting aliens) 119

Spider-Man friendly neighborhood
   Super Hero 92–93, 94

Stark, Tony a.k.a. Iron Man 61, 88, 89,
   112

Stegron, the Dinosaur Man 94–95

Storm, X-Men member 117

supernatural forces 44, 59, 66, 87, 90

super-soldier serum 70–71, 86

S'yan, T'Challa's uncle 52

Thor, Asgardian god 12, 35, 102–103,
   118

trials grueling tests to become Black
   Panther 22, 27, 43, 62

T'Chaka, T'Challa's dad 25, 38, 4
   killed by Klaue! 25, 72

Ultron, robotic villain 35, 78–79,
   114–115

Van Dyne, Janet 108–109

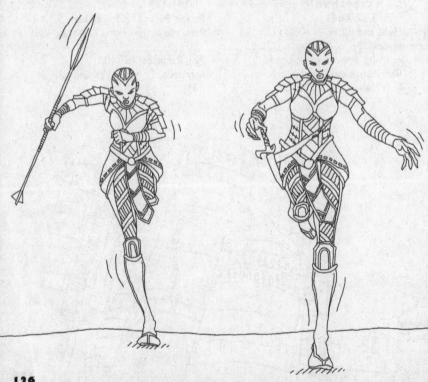

Vibranium, magical space metal 11, 18, 32–35, 61, 66, 101
    from a crashed meteorite 18–19, 66–67
    powering battlesuits 30–31, 97, 100
    powering weapons 48, 61, 75
    shield 33, 61, 87
    and thieving villains 25, 64, 72, 73, 78, 115
Vision, android super hero 114–115
Wakanda, Black Panther's homeland 10–11, 49, 56–57
    attacks on 24, 64, 72, 75, 81, 117
    the history bit 18–19, 20–21, 58–67, 74
    and magical Vibranium 18–19, 24, 34, 62, 64, 66
    royal family of 38–41, 52, 63
    snazzy high-tech inventions 8, 16, 41, 61, 100–101
Wasp, shrinking Super Hero 108–109, 119
Wilson, Sam a.k.a. Falcon 96
W'Kabi, Wakandan security chief 51
X-Men, powerful team of Super Heroes 117
Zenzi, mind-reading villain 81
Zola, Arnim evil scientist 71, 81
Zuri, giant Wakanda warrior 53

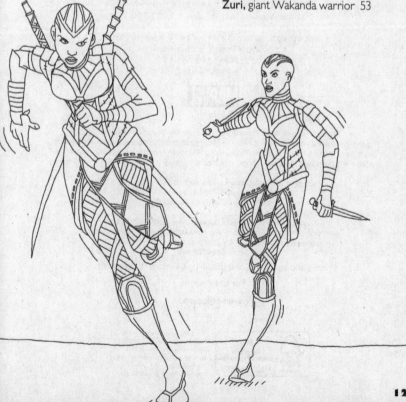

Penguin
Random
House

Editor Julia March
Project Editor Shari Last
Senior Editor Emma Grange
Project Art Editor Jon Hall
Senior Designers Nathan Martin, Mark Penfound, and Clive Savage
Managing Editor Sarah Harland
Managing Art Editor Vicky Short
Senior Pre-Production Producer Jennifer Murray
Senior Producers Mary Slater and Louise Daly
Publisher Julie Ferris
Art Director Lisa Lanzarini
Publishing Director Mark Searle

Illustrations by Dan Crisp and Jon Hall

DK would like to thank Kayla Dugger for editorial help
and Elizabeth Dowsett for the index.

First American Edition, 2020
Published in the United States by DK Publishing
1450 Broadway, Suite 801, New York, NY 10018

Page design Copyright © 2021 Dorling Kindersley Limited
DK, a Division of Penguin Random House LLC
21 22 23 24 25 10 9 8 7 6 5 4 3 2
005–316355–Sept/2020

©2021 MARVEL

A catalog record for this book is available from the Library of Congress.
ISBN 978-1-4654-9159-6 (Paperback)
ISBN 978-1-4654-8999-9 (Hardback)

DK books are available at special discounts when purchased in bulk for
sales promotions, premiums, fund-raising, or educational use. For details, contact:
DK Publishing Special Markets, 1450 Broadway, Suite 801, New York, NY 10018
SpecialSales@dk.com

Printed and bound in Great Britain by Clays Ltd, Elcograf S.p.A.

For the curious

www.dk.com